W9-CUB-237

1/31/13
#9.99

TOMMY TWICEBORN

An Incredible journey into past life inspired by
a true story of reincarnation

Published by
www.Nightowlscribe.com

AMEENA A SAEED

Tommy Twiceborn: An incredible Journey into past life inspired by a true life story of reincarnation

Copyright C 2012 Ameena A Saeed. All rights reserved. No part of this book may be used or reproduced in any manner whatsoever without prior permission except for quotations in critical reviews.

Published by www.nightowlscribe.com
For more information go to www.tommytwiceborn.com

First Edition 2012

Library of Congress control Number: 2012938655
ISBN: 0985186100
ISBN 13: 9780985186104

I dedicate this book to my mother, to all mothers

PREFACE

How long should one keep a story buried inside one's memory before it fades into oblivion or gets shredded by the mundane chores of life that seem so important in that moment. I have been haunted by this real life event for over thirty five years. It remained a puzzle, a question mark that would forever remain without an answer.

A young boy Vishnu, about twelve years old, in my brother's school in New Delhi , India began to talk about his past life as Shiva, (names changed to protect identity). His narrative was unambiguous and convincing. But the content was to say the least bizarre. Even in a country like India where reincarnation, Karma and past life are woven into the fabric of their culture, Vishnu's narrative was not taken seriously. He would talk about how as Shiva lived with his parents in a three story building. One day while flying a kite on his terrace, he slipped and fell to his death.

Students relished his story but no one thought much of it until one day a reporter from a local newspaper got wind of the tale and decided to investigate Vishnu's claim of his past life. The reporter searched for the neighborhood that Vishnu had described. He asked around if there had been an accident in that area some thirteen years ago where a young boy may have fallen to his death.

The reporter could not believe his luck when he located a busy neighborhood where people corroborated the story of Vishnu. Indeed there has been an accident, some thirteen years ago where a young boy had died in a kite flying accident. The parents of the deceased boy could not be reached because they had moved without leaving a forwarding address.

Then the story took a bizarre twist. While the reporter was still investigating the story, Vishnu who lived in a high rise apartment with his parents, fell to his death in a freak accident. Vishnu was exactly the same age as Shiva when he died.

The story has haunted me since. It left many questions unanswered. Is reincarnation a possibility? If so why do some remember their past lives while others don't? Should we even concern ourselves with these possibilities in the era of iPod and instant gratification?

There are some who have gone beyond superficial curiosity to committed research. And I want to acknowledge all those who inspired me to write this novel. Ian Stevenson a Canadian biochemist and professor of psychiatry was fascinated by the paranormal and specially reincarnation. He logged 55,000 miles and some 5,000 interviews mostly with children, all over the world, who spoke cogently of their previous lives. He wrote several books on the subject that include 'Twenty cases Suggestive of Reincarnation' and 'Where Reincarnation and Biology Intersect.'

My protagonist Tommy Stevenson is a tribute to Dr. Ian Stevenson.

Carol Bowman author, lecturer and therapist known for her book 'Children's Past Lives.' She has been involved in studying cases of reincarnation for over twenty years.

And of course Dr. Brian Weiss, a psychiatrist, hypnotist and healer , author of 'Many Lives Many Masters' and 'Through Time Into Healing' where he combines wisdom, compassion with scientific analysis.

ACKNOWLEDGEMENT

I would like to acknowledge my friends who encouraged me all these years to continue and finish my project. I thank the higher powers for friendship, for unanswered questions and the blessings of uncertainty that keeps creativity flowing.

CHAPTER 1

On a muggy and warm September afternoon, the sixth graders at Thurgood Marshall Elementary school diligently took notes as the teacher, Ms. Stooksberry, wrote on the blackboard in her neat handwriting. Students were trying to get back into the discipline of learning after the long summer holiday. The absolute silence in the classroom was typical since Ms. Stooksberry was a stickler for discipline.

According to some students, Ms. Stooksberry was born with a book in one hand and chalk in the other. The school authorities had been gently persuading her to retire and make room for fresh talent. However, she was only fifty-five and in no hurry to say good-bye to her first love, teaching. Besides, it takes time to remove an icon.

Tommy, Pete, Johnny, and Megan, known as the Furtive Four by their peers, exchanged meaningful glances. Johnny, the leader of the group, raised a finger, signaling his friends to wait for the right moment. He had a mop of brown, wavy hair on a baby face with freckles; it made for a sharp contrast to his big physique.

"The capitol of the state of California is Sacramento," Mrs. Stooksberry said in her stern voice. She turned around and peered through her rimless glasses at the silent class. Sometimes a very quiet bunch of twenty-five sixth graders could be unsettling. She cast one satisfied glance at the class and turned back to the board.

Tommy looked at her out of the corner of his eye. She did not suspect anything. Her neatly made, salt-and-pepper bun sat majestically on her head, reminding him of the dome of the Capitol Building in Sacramento. She was so good at history that she looked part of it.

Tommy, a skinny eleven-year-old, had big blue eyes on an angular face that exuded kindness and innocence. His hair was a mix of dark brown with a touch of red. His appearance reminded people of his father, Frank Stevenson. Tommy was articulate with an inquisitive mind. He not only came up with new ideas for pranks but also was able to finish his assignments on time. He had to watch what he ate, especially when it came to candy, soda, and fries. He had been living with juvenile diabetes since the age of six.

"Now," Johnny whispered.

Tommy passed his pencil box to Megan, Johnny's hazel-eyed, blonde twin sister. She was the most sensible member of the Furtive Four. She brought order and calm when the male members of the group could not agree on something crucial.

Megan took four pencils from the box and held them in her fist so they all looked equal in length. She held out her closed hand to the group, who in a random selection pulled out a pencil each. The first three were all full-size pencils. Johnny got the half pencil, which he gleefully showed off to the others. Megan nudged Tommy, who passed the pencil box to Johnny.

Johnny opened Tommy's pencil box and gently took out a six-and-half-inch-long leopard gecko with a forked tail. He caressed the reptile fondly. "Dear friend, time to play."

The gecko, Leo, belonged to Tommy. It was a gift from his father Frank, a mountain climber, who had brought the gecko back from a climbing expedition in Pakistan on the border of Afghanistan. The gecko must have gotten in his carry-on luggage and survived in the warmth of his clothes. It was a special kind of gecko, found only in dry, extreme climates.

Tommy was surprised to learn that there were websites and chat rooms devoted to gecko owners with enough material to write a manual on Leopard geckos. Tommy had learned to feed the gecko with mealworms from the pet store and to let him hunt an occasional cricket. Male geckos were territorial, Tommy had learned, just like men. When it came to wooing a desirable female gecko, two male geckos would tear each other apart, just like humans. By having an unusual pet and doing so much research on it, Tommy had become a source of admiration and envy to his friends and classmates.

"Do it," Tommy whispered to Johnny, who quietly placed Leo on Lisa's desk behind him. For a few moments, the gecko stood on its tiny hind legs at the head of Lisa's desk, polishing its large, protruding eyeballs with a long, snakelike tongue. Lisa was so engrossed in writing that she did not notice anything odd. There was nothing to nibble, so Leo jumped to the floor and looked around, his forked tail swaying in the air.

Pete, the nerd of the group, wearing glasses larger than his face, did not like practical jokes. He ignored Leo and buried his head in the book. As long as there was quiet in the class, he was safe, or so he thought.

Leo jumped toward Tommy and looked up expectantly.

"Pick it up," Johnny whispered fiercely. He had lost his chance to mess up the class because of stupid Leo and dim-witted Lisa, who did not notice anything odd. Tommy picked up Leo gently by the belly, turned around, and placed him on Sandy's desk, behind him. Johnny, who had a soft spot for Sandy, squirmed. Sandy, who was forever alert except in academic matters, noticed the impertinent gecko standing on its hind legs on her history book. She let out a gut-wrenching scream and began to cry as she found herself fixed to her chair and faced with an ogling gecko, still wiping his lashless eyes with his tongue. Some students gasped in shock while others cringed and moved away from the reptile.

Sandy and Leo held each other in a deep stare until Johnny, unable to bear seeing her in pain, reached out and grabbed Leo by his forked tail. Leo abruptly slipped out of Johnny's grip and landed in the middle of the class.

Any remaining order in the classroom was suddenly shattered as kids began to yell, scream, and throw things off their desks. The class was tossing poor Leo around, and Tommy was panicking. The last time something similar had happened Leo's long tail had come off.

The chaos was at its height as some kids took to standing on chairs and desks to stay out of the reach of the lizard. In the meantime, Leo had disappeared in the mayhem.

"Quiet. Sit down, everyone;" hollered the teacher. "What's the matter?"

Silence descended on the room as the sixth graders settled on their chairs and stared at Ms. Stooksberry in stupefied silence. Leo, unable to handle the chaos of the sixth graders, had ended up sitting majestically on top of Ms. Stooksberry's bun. The meticulous Pete wondered how Leo had gotten up so far, and he hid his face behind the American history book. Megan giggled; Tommy and Johnny let out a guffaw and immediately covered their faces.

Ms. Stooksberry followed the gaze of the students and heard a strange chittering sound coming from the top of her head. In the next moment, she realized that whatever had caused the commotion was sitting on her head. She screamed and whacked her head with both hands. Her bun came unraveled as her motions lobbed Leo back in the class, shattering the students' silence once more.

Ten minutes later, Ms. Stooksberry, holding Tommy's hand, dragged him to the counselor's room. It was not the first time she had caught the prankster playing tricks in the class.

"You will be appropriately punished for this, Thomas Stevenson," Ms. Stooksberry said rigidly as she marched through the hall.

"I swear, Ms. Stooksberry, it wasn't for you. It was for the lunch lady. We're tired of her cooking," Tommy protested.

"That's gratifying indeed. You're a great storyteller. Now you have detention for two days."

"Oh please, Ms. Stooksberry, can I get a rain check? I might have to attend Grandma's funeral tomorrow. I've never been to a funeral. Please," he pleaded.

"When did your Grandma die?" Ms. Stooksberry stopped abruptly.

"Anytime now. She's in hospice care. Mom said Grandma wouldn't make it to the evening. Then we can have the funeral tomorrow."

CHAPTER 2

It was eight in the evening, and there was still light in the sky. Carol, Tommy's mother, emerged from her bedroom, ready to go to work. She was a fragile-looking blonde-haired woman in her mid-thirties who worked nights as a nurse in the local hospital. She was a single mother, and she looked anxious and overwhelmed from the demands of her job in addition to taking care of her son.

"Mom, how's Grandma?" Tommy asked as Carol reached the door.

"The hospice facility called; the life support is working," Carol said.

"That means I have detention tomorrow," he said softly.

"What?" Carol asked.

"Nothing Mom. You take care of yourself and take a break whenever you can." Tommy kissed his mother. It bothered him she had to work nights.

"Of course, honey. Remember to take your insulin shot at nine sharp. Lock the door and don't watch TV after ten. I'll call to say good night."

"Mom, you don't have to call me. I will be in bed by ten," Tommy reassured her. "I'm a big boy."

"I'll call at ten." Carol kissed him and looked around to see if everything was in place.

She did not like leaving Tommy alone at night while she worked the hospital, but the neighborhood was safe and people were friendly. On this warm, still night, she would have preferred to sprawl on the sofa with popcorn and watch a mystery movie with her son.

Carol now looked far different from the spunky, attractive cheerleader she had been when she married her childhood sweetheart Frank Stevenson. Then misfortune struck, Frank had been a professional mountain climber. On his last expedition, he had climbed on the K2 mountain range in Pakistan, which was an extension of Mount Everest, the highest mountain in the world. He had been leading a group of climbers at base camp, waiting for the weather to clear so they could scale the most challenging peak the next morning. However, as fate would have it, they never made it to the summit. All fourteen climbers, along with Frank, were lost after a deadly earthquake devastated the region on October 8, 2005.

In the newspaper reports that detailed the tragedy, Carol and Tommy learned of the dangers that Frank had undertaken year after year along with other climbers.

The Karakoram Range consisted of the jagged cluster of razor-sharp ridges known as K2. The gigantic glacier below had been moving a few inches every year for millennia. Climbers and photographers described the area beyond the ridges as an ocean of snow with yawning chasms that were like death traps. There was no margin of error. That grandiose range of mountains had snuffed out the lives of many adventurous climbers in the past. Yet, Frank and other climbers had sworn by the beauty of those majestic mountain peaks. The thrill of climbing had no equal, according to Tommy's father.

When the earthquake struck on that fateful morning, the region's children were in school, the women at home, and the men at work. The survivors talked of hearing a huge rumbling noise at first, followed by the shaking of those colossal, unreachable peaks. Then the devastation let loose. Boulders as massive as cathedral domes and granite slabs as large as football fields rolled down under the weight of gravity. Within minutes, the picturesque landscape had changed into a disaster zone.

Nearly 250,000 people had died, many of them buried under the rubble of their houses, crushed by falling boulders, or consumed by moving gorges. None of the party of climbers made it. Rescue workers believed that all fourteen were buried alive under tons of debris. The mounds of boulders and hundreds of feet of snow, caused by the shaking and rumbling of the earthquake, stamped out any sign of life. The search parties scoured the rugged mountains for weeks but found no sign of survivors. In fact, the whole mountain range where the climbers had been resting on that fateful day had changed in topography. The disaster squeezed the valley into oblivion and changed the course of streams. What had once been small houses looked like piles of pebbles.

Tommy and Carol did not have a grave for Frank because the body was never recovered, but they did have a service in the church. Tommy, who was nine years old and in fourth grade at the time, felt angry with God. It was bad enough to lose his father; it was worse to be denied a family shrine. At the same time, not having a grave for his father made him feel sometimes that his father was still alive. Tommy did not know that Carol had similar thoughts.

Carol had to finish her course work and take whatever job was available. The insurance company had helped her with mortgage payments for a year. However, it had been eighteen months since then, and she was back on her own, working full time, paying bills, and taking care of Tommy, who was now the center of her universe.

"Tommy is a responsible eleven-year-old, but he still needs supervision," Carol said to Nicole, the colleague she was giving a ride. "He had to become a man overnight."

"He never talks about his father?" Nicole asked.

"I have seen him talking to his father's photograph."

"Oh, that's intense. He never complains?"

"Never. Not once has he complained or whined about the loss. It was a joint decision because we can never fix the past," Carol said sadly, as she steered into the hospital parking lot.

Life for mother and son was back on an even keel, but the sorrow and uncertainty continued to trouble them both. Sometimes the two would go out for a movie or a boat ride, but there was always emptiness between them that would never be filled.

After Carol left the house, Tommy locked the door from inside and looked at his watch. It was nearly eight, and there was still light outside. In one hour,

Johnny, Megan, and Pete would be crawling out of their respective bedrooms to assemble at the front gate of the local cemetery. They were going to build a small fire, roast marshmallows, and wait for ghosts, whom they believed came out only on a full-moon night. Good thing he had completed his homework in school.

At nine, Tommy called his mother and said, "Mom, I finished my homework and I'm going to sleep early, so you don't need to call me at ten."

"Did you take your shot?"

"I'm taking it right now," Tommy said into the speakerphone, inserting the needle in the bottle of insulin. He drew 10 cc of the cloudy liquid in the syringe. He tapped the syringe to make sure there were no air bubbles. He then rubbed a small area on his belly with a swab and inserted the needle. He had learned to give himself a shot twice a day after he got juvenile diabetes. However, each time, the prick of the needle was an uncomfortable sensation. "There, I'm done. Good night, Mom."

"Good night, hon."

With his homework, mother, and insulin shot out of the way, Tommy put on his jacket. From the garage, he picked up his adventure backpack, which included a flashlight, a quick snack, a bottle of soda, a rope, and a Swiss Army knife.

"C'mon, Leo, let's go! Maybe we can find you a girlfriend," Tommy said to the wide-eyed Leo who swished his forked tail back and forth in excitement. Tommy slipped him into his shirt pocket and left the house, carefully shutting the door behind him, got his bike, and rode down the hill to meet his friends at the cemetery. Maybe they would see some ghosts if they were lucky.

There was a slight chill as the evening temperature dropped. It was supposed to be a full moon, but a blanket of haze hid the sky. Tommy rode to where Pete, Megan, and Johnny were waiting for him at the gate. The cemetery was quiet and melancholy except for the sound of a coyote in the distance or the crickets on the ground. It was not breezy, but even the slightest movement in the air caused the leaves to rustle, and it sounded creepy. As they walked inside, the rows and rows of gravestones sent an eerie message to all four friends. The dead surrounded them, literally.

The four chose a spot under a large tree. They collected dry leaves and twigs, lit a small fire, and began to roast marshmallows. The roasted marshmallows remained untouched on a paper plate. It was difficult to eat with a gloomy sky above and dead people around.

Pete kept craning his neck and looking over his shoulder. His nervousness was obvious. A certified nerd he had joined Johnny's group because he wanted to shake off the boring image that stood between him and fun.

"Don't worry, Pete; ghosts can scare us but not harm us." Megan sensed his discomfort.

"Do you think we'll see any tonight?" Pete asked anxiously. He liked Megan and Tommy. They were easy on him.

"I hope so," Johnny said gruffly.

Pete looked around again. He would rather be reading a scary story in bed than having a hair-raising experience among the cold and dreary graves at night.

"I hope it's a girl ghost." Megan said, looking at the three male faces. Sometimes she missed having another girl in the group.

"Girl ghosts will be stuffy and frail." Johnny grunted.

"Really, Johnny, if I'm not mistaken, Megan has gotten you out of trouble more times than you've helped her." Tommy said feeding Leo a piece of marshmallow,

"We have to be nice; ghosts can be nasty." Pete said nervously.

"Don't worry. I'll take care of them." Johnny assertively touched his BB gun.

"What're you gonna do, drumhead? Kill the ghost?" Tommy laughed.

"I don't like cemeteries." Pete said as he finally found an opening.

"Grow up and be a man." Johnny said

Leo, who was standing near the fire, looked excited as another lizard slithered past.

"Leo needs a girlfriend," Megan said with empathy.

"A man's got to have a partner," Johnny said pompously.

"How do you know Leo is not a female?" Pete, as usual, demanded explanation of everything.

"I had him examined at the pet shop, and they said he was male. The area underneath his tail is bulky. Females have a small pouch there," Tommy said proudly.

They all looked at Leo affectionately. The large pupils of his enormous eyes shifted wildly left and right. The reflection of fire in his eyes was something to behold. His long, slick tongue kept reaching his eyeballs. Suddenly Leo jumped, skipped past the fire, and before Tommy could catch him, Leo was standing several feet from the group.

"Megan, grab him!" Tommy tried to seize Leo, who jumped farther away from the gang. "Don't grab him by the tail. It might come off. I don't want a gecko with three tails," said Tommy anxiously, reminding everyone, that Johnny had once pulled Leo by his tail and a piece of the tail had come off, much to Tommy's angst. Leo had eaten his own severed piece of tail. Two weeks later, the friends were astonished to see Leo grow an extension of his tail. Now Leo had a forked tail and was more special.

CHAPTER 3

The haze still covered the full moon, and the darkness in the cemetery was dreary. With the powerful beams of their flashlights, the four searched frantically for Leo. The free-spirited gecko either was attracted to a female lizard or had gone after a cricket meal, or both.

"We'll never find him in this darkness," Pete said anxiously.

"We will, Pete. Don't you worry." Megan, as usual, calmed his nerves.

Just then, they heard the familiar chittering sound of the gecko.

"There he is," Tommy said as the beam of his flashlight caught Leo proudly standing on his hind legs atop a gravestone. He had a cricket in his mouth. Tommy, Megan, Johnny, and Pete surrounded Leo, and Tommy carefully got Leo's belly in between his thumb and two fingers. Leo swished his tail fiercely in the air, a sign that his hunting trip had been successful. Tommy carefully put the gecko back in his shirt pocket while Leo nibbled at his favorite dinner. The full moon sparkled from the ink-blue sky as it slithered out from behind the dark clouds.

"Hey! Look here." Megan's eye caught something odd. She pointed at the row of three graves where they had grabbed Leo. The inscriptions on the three gravestones read Philip, Mary, and Sean Butler.

"Father, mother and holy s…" Pete tried to be funny. He always did that when he was scared.

"Son. They all died the same day, May 11, 1995," said Tommy.

"Maybe it was an accident," Johnny said with authority.

"Yeah, unless they were all on a suicide mission just for the fun of it." Tommy said sarcastically. He occasionally liked to take a dig at Johnny. "Of course, man. If the whole family died on the same day it *had* to be an accident." "I wonder if the Butler family lived in this town," Megan reflected.

"If they did, there's only one elementary school in San Felipe," Pete added.

"Yeah, our school." Johnny interjected.

"Not bad for a B-minus average." Tommy took one more dig at Johnny. It was dark, and there were no ghosts in sight.

"There is George Washington Elementary across the lake," Pete said thoughtfully.

"I've an idea. One of us will pretend to be Sean's ghost and visit his old school," Johnny said excitedly. Everyone was quiet. Johnny's talent lay not in thinking up original ideas but in executing them. Tommy and Pete were more cerebral, while Megan was good at refining the plans and rounding off the edges. This was an interesting and original idea for the newest prank, and they were surprised that it came from Johnny.

"That's cool, Johnny," said Pete.

"Not a ghost, but a reincarnation of Sean Butler," Megan said.

"What's reincarnation?" Johnny asked.

"It means you've lived a life before and are born again," Tommy said.

"That would be fun. We can actually do some research on Sean Butler and on reincarnation," Pete said excitedly. He wanted to get out of the cemetery and into the library.

"Yeah," Johnny yawned. "Only a nerd like you would like to pore over books in a library." However, it was Johnny's idea, and they were all going to work at it. He felt like a leader again.

"How about the reincarnation of Sean Butler visiting his old school," Tommy thought aloud.

"And bothering Ms. Stooksberry." Megan laughed at the thought.

"Who's going to be Sean?" Pete asked the million-dollar question.

"Since it was my idea, I think…" Then Johnny was disappointed because Megan, according to rules, took out three pencils from the pencil box; one was already broken in half. She turned around and adjusted them in her grip so they all looked equal. She then faced the three boys and held out her hand. Pete pulled out a pencil and was relieved to see he was not the chosen one. Johnny frowned as he saw Tommy pull out the broken pencil.

Leo nibbled at his cricket while the three friends stared at Tommy. The friends smiled in anticipation. It would be fun playing their newest prank in school.

"Let's do some research on reincarnation before we begin to psych people out," Pete said excitedly.

"Sean died a month before his twelfth birthday, which was on June fifteenth." Pete read the inscription under the flashlight.

"Now that is strange. June fifteenth is your birthday, too, Tommy," Megan said, reading the inscription herself.

"What a coincidence," said Pete.

"Hello, Sean Butler. Welcome to the world again." Megan playfully extended her hand to greet Tommy. The friends laughed, even Leo happily swished his forked tail.

Suddenly, the wailing sound of a coyote in the distance startled them. A sudden gust of wind lifted loose dirt off the ground and put out the small fire they had built. The moon crept behind a menacing dark cloud again, and the cemetery plunged into total darkness. The shadow of swaying willow trees in the evening wind gave the impression of angry ghosts advancing toward the group. The graves looked like an army of midgets threateningly moving along with them.

"Run for your life; they're coming for us"!" Pete let out a terrified shriek. Megan and Tommy scooped up their backpacks, Johnny grabbed his BB gun, and everyone darted toward the gate, running and stumbling as fast as they could, with the nonathletic Pete in the lead.

⟨⊗⟩

Tommy was ready for school. He had showered and put on his clothes and slung his backpack across his shoulder. Carol yawned, holding a steaming cup of coffee. She was going to hit the hay for a good six hours.

"Mom, you look so tired. When are they going to take you off the graveyard shift?" Tommy said, pouring milk on his cereal.

"Soon, they've assured me; next month, maybe." Carol yawned and rubbed her eyes again. "Before I forget, let me check your glucose," She reached for the box containing testing strips and needles. She put a fresh needle on the pen, cleaned the top of Tommy's middle finger with an antiseptic swab, and gently pressed the pen to his finger. A small drop of blood appeared. She then scooped the drop onto the strip and waited five seconds. "One hundred and two," she said, looking satisfied.

"Mom, do I have to do this all my life?" Tommy asked with a long face.

"There is good news, honey; with stem cell technology they may be able to rejuvenate your pancreas to produce insulin on its own."

"When will that be possible?"

"You're lucky, sweetheart. In a few years, you may be rid of type one diabetes forever," she said, putting away the testing kit in the kitchen drawer. "Let's hope for the best."

"Okay, time for me to go. Mom, please don't do any chores after I'm gone. I'll help you when I get back," Tommy said.

"Thanks, sweetheart. I promise I'll rest." She kissed him on his cheek. "Now run along."

Twenty minutes later when Tommy reached school, Ms. Stooksberry was standing at the gate. He tried to avoid her, but she marched over to him.

"Tommy, I need to talk to you."

"Ms. Stooksberry, I'm sorry. I was sure that Grandma was going to die, but she didn't."

"You need to return home," Ms. Stooksberry said, gently touching Tommy's shoulder. "Your mother called."

CHAPTER 4

t was a bright, sunny day with a gentle, warm wind, but the mood was somber at the cemetery. Tommy and Carol were dressed for his grandma's funeral. Tommy's blue eyes and brown hair with a tinge of red were a sharp contrast to the black suit he wore.

For Tommy, it was the second visit to the cemetery in two days. He looked around. The willow trees looked elegant and the graves somber, unlike last night when everything had looked sinister and threatening. *What a difference a day and night could make!* Tommy thought of last night.

"Oh, Carol, I'm so sorry. It's terrible to lose two loved ones in a span of eighteen months." A woman from the church hugged Carol and kissed Tommy.

I wish she would not bring it up, Tommy thought angrily, looking at his mother who was trying to put up a brave front. *Grandma was eighty-six and had been seriously ill for a couple of years. It's not the same as losing a young, adventurous father.*

"Don't worry, Mom, I'll always be there to take care of you," he whispered, trying to look strong even though he felt anxious and vulnerable.

"I know, love. I trust you." Carol hugged him affectionately. They both placed flowers on the freshly dug grave. Both were thinking of Frank. He missed his father terribly but put up a brave front for his mother because he felt he had to be the man in her life.

"Tommy, dear, hold my hand." Carol sniffled as they stood before the freshly dug grave where Grandma was going to be laid to rest.

While the ceremony was in progress, the three Butler graves in the distance distracted Tommy. After the funeral rites, while Carol was engaged in conversation with friends, he walked to the three Butler graves and stood staring at them.

A few minutes later, Carol walked up to him and gently pulled on his jacket sleeve. "Let's go, Tommy." Holding hands, they walked to the exit.

"Whose grave was that?"

"Mine." Tommy's inaudible response was lost as a couple said their good-byes to Carol.

"You said something, honey?"

"Nah." Tommy shrugged his shoulders.

CHAPTER 5

To their surprise, the Furtive Foursome found books, articles, websites, and online videos about reincarnation and past-life experiences. Barring Johnny, who found it difficult to sit still on the computer, the subject fascinated them. After completing their research, they met to exchange information. Armed with stories that were stranger than fiction, they sat around the dining table in Tommy's house.

Pete started first. "In Eastern philosophy, they believe that all humans are reincarnated." "That means they have lived a life before and are reborn. Their karma decides where and how they are reborn."

"What's karma?" asked Johnny

"Something similar to as you sow, so shall you reap. It's a Hindu concept borrowed by the Buddhists. We in the West don't give much importance to it, but it's a big thing in India where people actively perform certain rituals to make their next life better." Pete read from his spiral notebook

"Now this is a definite case of reincarnation in America. A six-year-old boy in a southern state in the USA claimed he was a navy fighter pilot who died during World War II after the Japanese shot down his plane. For his age, he had detailed information on fighter planes and dogfight in the sky. Everyone was surprised since the only programs he watched were children's programs. Later it was confirmed from documentary evidence that indeed a young fighter pilot, fitting the description the boy had provided, had died in a crash during the Second World War." Tommy too had done his research.

"In 1957, in England, a man lost his two daughters, ages six and eleven, in an automobile accident. Later his pregnant wife had twin daughters who not only looked like their two deceased daughters but also had the same birthmarks. At a very early age, the toddlers were able to identify areas they had visited in their previous life and asked for toys about which they should have had no information," Megan told them.

Silence filled the room as all four absorbed the fascinating stories of past lives.

"And there is this four-year-old English boy who had a cyst in his throat. The doctors said they had to remove the cyst before it became cancerous. The boy had been having nightmares about cold, damp, rainy weather all his childhood. One day, he remembered an event from his past life. He was a soldier in France fighting on the front in the First World War. On a cold and rainy day during a gun battle, the young soldier was shot through his throat. He felt the blood filling his mouth and remembered dying at age eighteen." Pete narrated this one. "Miraculously, after he remembered that event, his nightmares stopped. The cyst in his throat also disappeared, leaving the doctors baffled."

"Wow," a spellbound Johnny said. He wished, he too had done some reading.

"Now listen to my favorite story of reincarnation," Tommy said excitedly. "This one has been haunting me. It's about an eleven-year-old fifth grader called Vishnu in New Delhi, India. One day he began to talk about his past life as Shiva to his classmates. He vividly remembered his home in the city, his parents, and the manner of his death. He said in his past life, while flying a kite on his third-floor terrace, he fell and died. A local reporter, who began to investigate Vishnu's claim, picked up the story.

"To his surprise, the reporter found that indeed, about thirteen years ago, there had been a tragic accident in a certain neighborhood. A boy called Shiva had tripped and fallen off his third-floor terrace." Tommy paused.

"The reporter began to look for the deceased boy's parents; they had moved to an unknown location. Soon there was a bizarre twist to the episode. Vishnu, who lived with his present parents in a high-rise building, in a freak accident, fell from his window and died again." Tommy looked at his friends, who were enthralled by the story.

Ms. Stooksberry's civic education class was in progress. The students were engrossed in the presentation as she changed the slides on the overhead projector. All sixth graders were attentively listening to her, except Tommy, who stared at the closed window. Ms. Stooksberry pointed at the picture of Ryan White.

"Ryan White, who was diagnosed with AIDS at age thirteen, was the victim of prejudice because people thought AIDS was contagious. They thought one could get the deadly disease by being in the same room. Ryan White fought against this stigma until his death at age sixteen. Today he lives amongst us in spirit." She noticed Tommy looking out the window.

"Tommy, you're not paying attention. Can you repeat what I just said?"

"Yes. Sean Butler, who died twelve years ago, lives both in body and spirit among us," Tommy said somberly.

"Who's Sean Butler?" A surprised Ms. Stooksberry peered through her rimless glasses.

"I'm Sean Butler. Yesterday at the cemetery, I saw my grave," Tommy said flatly.

Silence filled the room. Some kids looked puzzled while others rolled their eyes. The trio, Megan, Johnny, and Pete snickered knowingly. Ms. Stooksberry was still trying to decipher the meaning of that response when the glass window opened and slammed shut due to a sudden gust of wind. Everyone was startled. The trio chuckled. Tommy continued to stare out the window. Megan made a thumbs-up sign to Johnny and Pete. Their plan was working.

Ms. Stooksberry was not amused. At the end of class, she led Tommy down the hall to the counselor.

"I know your grandmother died last week, but that is no reason—" Ms. Stooksberry checked herself. That was a good reason for anyone to be upset. "I'm going to recommend grief counseling for you."

"Ms. Stooksberry, you're one of the oldest teachers here," Tommy said. "Do you remember a student by the name of Sean Butler?"

"I don't remember anyone called Sean Butler, and don't you try to divert my attention." She marched Tommy toward the counselor's office.

"Oh, Ms. Stooksberry, you're no help! I'll just have to do my own research." Tommy sighed.

"Good morning, young man," Mr. Hackman said good-naturedly, even though he knew from the look on Ms. Stooksberry's face that Tommy was in trouble. He had come to know Tommy well by now. He had talked to him several times after the tragic death of his father. Hackman was of the opinion that Tommy had adjusted remarkably to that loss.

Inside the room, Tommy sat across from Counselor Hackman, who was short and portly and had a gray streak running through his dark hair. He looked kind and content with his life. His grin was sincere, and his eyes smiled before he did.

"Son, let me tell you that it is not unusual for people to go through behavioral changes when they lose a loved one," he said with compassion.

"Grandma hated me," said Tommy, looking at a bee buzzing over a flower vase.

"Death, graves, and funerals can unsettle people." Hackman ignored Tommy's response and continued. "Tell me, would you like me to talk to your mother. Our school district provides for group and individual grief counseling. I recommend a few sessions."

"Did you know a sixth grader called Sean Butler? He died about twelve years ago."

"No, Son. Besides, I've been in this school for only eight years."

"Where can I find a twelve-year-old phone book for Marina County?" Tommy asked, deep in thought.

"What will you do with it?" Hackman was puzzled.

"Research," Tommy replied.

"What kind of research?" Hackman asked.

"Can I go now?"

"Yes, but remember: if there is another incident of bad behavior, we'll have to talk to your mother." With that, Hackman let him go.

As Tommy left the room, he noticed the bee floating dead in the flower vase.

CHAPTER 6

"Let's look at the Marina county newspapers of May 11, 1995, on the microfiche," Tommy said to Megan. They were in the public library's back room.

"What's a microfiche?" asked Megan.

"Old documents, newspapers, and entire journals are reduced to photographic images about one twenty-fifth of the original size and stored in microfilms. It involves less labor, more efficiency, and it's easy to retrieve old documents. We run this film reel in the microfiche machine that enlarges these micro images," Tommy said, feeding a microfilm in the bulky machine and began to scan the newspaper dated May 11, 1995. "They are now digitizing old newspapers and texts. Soon we will have them on discs and can run them on our own computers."

"Cool. You know so much." Megan looked at him in awe as he rolled the film. But there was no news about the Butlers or any accident. They rolled the film to the next day and the next; again, there was no mention of any accident where three members of a family had died.

Disappointed, they left the library. At the Giant Burger restaurant, their favorite meeting point, Johnny and Pete joined them.

"No success," Megan said.

"Maybe we should go ask people if they remember the Butler family," said Johnny.

"Our parents might know something about the Butlers," Pete added.

"How about Dad's friend, Inspector Wilkinson? He could look into the police records and tell us about the Butler family. He's been on the police force for twenty years," said Megan, and everyone looked impressed.

"Inspector Wilkinson, now, why didn't *I* think of him?" said Johnny regretfully, licking ketchup from his fork.

"Maybe I'll have some news for you tomorrow," said Megan cheerfully, and they parted on an upbeat note.

At home, Tommy checked his mother's bedroom and found her sleeping soundly. He decided to do some chores before she woke up. He sorted and put the clothes in the washer, stacked dishes in the dishwasher, and quickly took out the clunky vacuum cleaner. He vacuumed the living room and the bathroom before he settled down to do his homework.

All that time, he thought about Sean Butler, a boy who died at age eleven. He felt strangely connected to Sean, with whom he shared a birthday. *Sean was around my age when he died,* Tommy reflected with a shiver.

Later that evening, the telephone rang. It was Johnny, and he had good news. Inspector Wilkinson was ready to talk to the foursome. They were supposed to meet him at his office tomorrow after school.

Next day, the four friends assembled outside the impressive gray stone building of the San Felipe Police Department. The urgency and seriousness of the people in uniform awed them. It turned out to be an important day for Johnny, who was fascinated with the blue uniforms.

"I'm going to join the police force after graduation." He had instantly found his life's calling.

"Really! You mean I'll be all by myself in college?" Megan faked a sigh of regret.

Inside the police station, the four friends were ushered into a busy office. Inspector Wilkinson was a big man with broad shoulders. He looked stern, but was so soft-spoken that Tommy wondered how he managed to arrest people. The inspector wanted to know why they needed the information they were requesting.

"Sir, we're doing an assignment on the history of accidents in the last thirteen years in San Felipe. But we couldn't get any information on the Butlers, who died in 1995," said Tommy. It was not the whole truth, but neither was it a lie.

"I looked into the database." The inspector pushed a file in front of them. "That was a slightly complicated case. They died on May 11, 1995, but their bodies were discovered about a week later. You should have looked up the newspapers dated May 18, 1995. That was the day the police report was filed."

"The plot thickens," Tommy muttered excitedly. "Thank you, sir, and the rest we can read in the newspapers."

"Are you sure?" the inspector asked, leading them to the door.

Outside, the excited foursome indulged in high fives.

"Bingo," Pete said, adjusting his glasses, "that takes us back to the library and more research."

"Let's meet after school tomorrow and go to the main library to try to unscramble the Butler mystery," Tommy said excitedly.

The next day after school, Tommy waited for his friends to join him, but Megan and Johnny said they had to accompany their mother to San Francisco, and Pete had to clean up the yard with his dad.

Tommy decided to go to the main library by himself. He knew his mother would sleep until five o'clock, so he had two hours by himself. Inside the library, he settled down and looked until he saw the images magnified on the screen that were dated May 18, 1995. There it was, splashed all over the headlines.

Butlers Pulled Out Of lake, Dead.

Where's Eleven Year Old Sean?

A tremor of excitement rippled through Tommy as he saw the picture of the Butler family for the first time. Sean had very short blond hair and a round face with deep-set blue-gray eyes and lots of freckles. A slight chill ran through Tommy's spine as he stared at Sean's picture. His heart beating with anticipation, Tommy read the rest of the news.

'The Butler family had been missing for seven days. No one noticed their absence because they had been on vacation. Philip Butler was a construction worker and his wife Mary a secretary in the same company. Sean Butler was a student at George Washington Elementary on the south side of Lake Blue Haven. Philip Butler's co-workers were concerned when the couple did not report to work after their vacation.'

The report continued on the next page.

'The police was informed, and they began a search. Two days later, a couple of people fishing in the lake noticed a wheel floating in the water. Police searched the waters and pulled out a van with the almost-unrecognizable bodies of Philip and Mary. The doors of the van were locked, and the handles had come off. It appears that they had parked their van at an incline. Detectives concluded that the van rolled back into the water or that the parking brakes failed and the Butlers had been unable to escape. No foul play was suspected, but the boy is still missing.'

His hands trembling with excitement, Tommy rolled the microfiche to next day's headline.

Where's Sean Butler?

Tommy found the answer in the headlines of next week, May 22, 1995.

Sean's Decomposed Body Recovered Downstream.

The veins in his head throbbing, Tommy read the story.

'Police pieced together the sequence of events. When the van carrying his parents rolled down the incline, Sean, who must have been outside, ran into the water to save his parents. He was not a swimmer and unsuccessfully struggled to open the doors of the van. The force of the current dragged him downstream, where he drowned. His body stayed entangled in the foliage where the search party found him later. Police identified him by his dental records.'

Tommy rolled the microfiche to the next day. The newspaper headline carried the report of the triple burial of the Butler family.

'The small town of San Felipe had not experienced anything so tragic in several decades. George Washington Elementary School, where Sean was a sixth grade student, closed for a day in remembrance of his premature death.'

Tommy leaned against his chair as he took out a sugarless candy bar from his pocket and chewed on it. He was exhausted with excitement. He looked at the clock; he should be home with his mother, who must be up by now and wondering about him. Leo, too, would be looking for him; it was time for the gecko to eat his mealworms. Tommy saved a small morsel of candy in the wrapper for Leo.

CHAPTER 7

The wind was beginning to get chilly during the day. Autumn was around the corner, and the leaves were slowly losing their green color. It was a day of great excitement for the Furtive Four. Research had given them unexpected results. They pored over the folder on the Butler family that Tommy had prepared. He had photocopied all the news reports from the microfiche and stacked them in chronological order.

"Good work, Tommy. There's nothing like research," said Pete.

"Bingo." Megan was pleased.

"Let's plan our next move," Johnny said, rubbing his hands.

"Okay, Tomorrow's half day at school. How about Pete and I go to the school district office tomorrow to search for Sean's grade report and other relevant material connected to his school?" said Tommy. He looked at Pete, who nodded.

"And you, Johnny and Megan, cycle down to the Butler house at 203 Maple Street and talk to the neighbors."

"I was just going to suggest that," said Johnny with disappointment. He did not like taking orders from others.

Next day after school, Pete and Tommy rode their bikes over to the school district office, which was only four blocks from the school. They entered the main hall and walked up to the curriculum secretary.

"We want to see the grades of the last thirteen years, ma'am," Tommy said.

"Hon,' why on earth would you want to see the records for thirteen years?" asked the very surprised secretary.

"We're working on a project to find out if the grade point average of elementary school kids has gone up or down in a decade." Tommy gave his practiced sentence with deadpan expression.

"We have to determine the quality of education and see if there need to be changes in the method of instruction." Pete rattled off the response he had prepared. It was sufficient to impress the secretary, who asked them to wait. A few minutes later, she brought a file of public records.

"You may photocopy what you need; we don't give the originals."

"It pays to be a nerd." Tommy smiled to Pete settling down in a chair. They quickly flipped the pages to George Washington Elementary School and scanned the names of sixth graders for the year 1995.

"Oh." They both let out a sigh of relief and looked at each other as they noticed Sean Butler's name.

Sean's overall GPA was 3.2; he was good in social studies but weak in math. Tommy's heart skipped a beat; the similarity was unsettling. They could not help reading the teacher's remarks: "Sean was a quiet and hardworking student. He was regular with his homework assignments. He did well in art classes." One teacher observed that Sean allowed other kids to bully him and that he needed help to build his self-esteem.

Both Pete and Tommy looked at the blank space near Sean's final semester grade.

Pete made a photocopy of the report, punched it with a three-hole puncher, and stacked it in the folder titled 'Sean Butler.'

"Wait till Megan and Johnny see this," Pete said with pride. He loved working at the library. It was less dreary than a cemetery.

On the other side of the city, Megan and Johnny were not that lucky. They rode on their bicycles to the address that had been the Butler family residence.

"I don't believe this," said Johnny to Megan, looking at the map in his hand.

They were surprised to find that there were no houses after 150 Maple Street. Instead, there was a children's park with a ravine beyond it.

"Let's go to city hall and find out what happened," Johnny said to Megan with a touch of irritation.

They cycled to the city hall, where the land officer was surprised to see sixth graders taking interest in the redevelopment of San Felipe.

"About ten years ago, during torrential rains, Maple Street and the surrounding neighborhood were flooded. Many houses had suffered severe damage. Since it was a low-lying area, the geologists recommended converting the area into a public park," the officer informed them.

"At least we know Sean's address," Megan said.

"That means no immediate neighbors." Johnny was visibly disappointed.

"C'mon, Johnny, we completed our assignment. That's important." Megan tried to lift Johnny's mood. "Now, let's go meet Pete and Tommy at Giant Burger and see what they have for us."

"We'll meet at the pool. Remember we have swimming lesson," Johnny said.

On the way back from the school district office, Pete talked animatedly about their research while Tommy remained in a reflective mood.

"What do you think, Tommy?" Pete said loudly.

"What?" Tommy was startled. He had not heard a word.

"How are we going to play it out?" asked Pete impatiently.

"Let's plan it together when we meet the rest," Tommy said thoughtfully.

"Yeah, in the pool. That's a great place to discuss our next plan of action," Pete said excitedly.

About twenty kids assembled in the after-school swimming class, taught by the hawkish instructor, Joe Black, and his assistant. Tommy and his friends had all signed up for the weekly swimming lessons.

Once in the pool, the four kids enjoyed sharing their experiences of that day.

"C'mon, Tommy, let's swim in the deep end," one of Tommy's classmates said.

"I don't want to," said Tommy brusquely.

"Oh, c'mon, don't be chicken," the classmate insisted, putting the inflatable tube around Tommy's neck and tried pulling him to the other part of the pool.

"Help, help me, or I'll die!" Tommy behaved in a manner like he never had before. He screamed, yelled, and struggled to get the tube off his neck.

"What's the matter, Son?" The swimming coach rushed to Tommy, but there was nothing wrong. Tommy was safe and standing in three feet of water.

"I cannot go into deep water," said Tommy anxiously. "He was trying to strangle me."

"No, he wasn't, Son. Besides, this is a life-saving flotation device; it cannot strangle you," the coach said, looking puzzled.

"You don't know that's how I died the last time. I saw my parents slipping into the lake and drowning. I don't want to die again."

Curious silence surrounded the pool. Johnny, Megan, and Pete smiled to each other. Tommy was doing better than expected.

"What's wrong with him?" the puzzled coach asked Tommy's friends.

"Coach, he thinks he is the reincarnation of Sean Butler, with whom he shares a birthday," Megan said with a deadpan face.

"Sean Butler, along with his dad and mom, died in a drowning accident around Lake Blue Haven in 1995," Johnny said as sadly as he could manage.

"Tommy Stevenson was born a year later with the spirit of Sean Butler and remembers everything of his past life." Pete faked a sigh.

"Step out, Son," The coach looked more puzzled. Were they playing a prank, or was the boy out of his mind? Either way, he had to separate Tommy from the others.

"Now tell me, what is it?" The coach faced Tommy seriously.

"I believe I'm Sean Butler, the sixth grader who died twelve years ago in a drowning accident." Tommy stared back at the coach.

While everyone looked on in disbelief at the turn of events, there was silence around the pool. No one noticed Pete, Megan, and Johnny exchanging smiles.

Next day Tommy was summoned to the counselor's office.

"Son, you're having a delayed reaction to your father's sudden death. I understand that, and I am recommending further counseling. We'll need your mother's permission for that," the counselor said seriously to Tommy.

"I don't want my mom to be involved in this," Tommy said firmly. "Please keep her out of it. I'll think of something."

"I need to know for sure: are you and your friends playing a practical joke?" The counselor peered at Tommy.

"I cannot say," Tommy said, looking out the window.

"You can't say because you don't know, or you can't say because you are bound by friendship?" Hackman asked seriously. "How is your diabetes? I would like to have the school nurse check your readings."

"I know high blood sugar can damage the nervous system, but mine is under control," Tommy responded irritably. "Please, let me go." As he opened the door, three bodies literally fell inside. The trio of Pete, Johnny, and Megan had pressed their ears hard against the door. Before the counselor could get up from his chair, the four kids had disappeared down the hallway.

Once they were out of the counselor's earshot, they burst out laughing. A few students passed by.

"Hey, you want to tell us all about this Sean Butler story?" a student asked eagerly.

"Well, if you treat us to chocolate sundaes with whipped cream, we might consider your request." Johnny, as usual, extracted full price for his labor.

"Chocolate sundaes are huge and expensive. We can share. You can buy two for the four of us." Megan felt bad for the curious classmates.

"I want my own." Johnny glared at her.

"Okay, let's meet after school." The students agreed.

"I didn't know it would go so well." Pete adjusted his glasses. His reputation as a nerd was beginning to diminish.

"We can have the whole school eating out of our collective hand." Johnny was enjoying the new bout of respect for his gang.

"Right now you're eating into their savings, Johnny. Gosh, a chocolate ice cream sundae. It seems we're all working to keep you overweight." Tommy took a friendly jibe at Johnny.

"I've earned it. Remember, Sean Butler was my idea. It's a pity I was not chosen to play Sean. We would have had a treat every day," Johnny said.

"We need new ideas," Megan said, rejoicing in the success of their plan.

"Let's go to the cemetery again tonight," said Tommy thoughtfully. "We might get some new ideas."

"No!" Pete reacted sharply. "Remember, it's a prank. We don't have to do the real thing. We can plan better in school or at the library."

"Chicken." Johnny looked at Pete disapprovingly. "You nearly could have earned the gold medal for a five-hundred-meter race when you dashed out of the cemetery the other day."

"We'll go this weekend," said Tommy decisively, not knowing why.

The days were getting shorter, and the evenings had a chill as the sleepy town of San Felipe prepared for fall. The East Coast was already experiencing early blizzards and power outages.

While Carol was in the shower, Tommy worked on his science assignment out of recycled materials. After doing research on the Internet, he had decided to make a periscope. He had two empty milk cartons, washed and dried. He cut off the slanted tops of each carton. Then he cut out a viewing hole on the bottom of each. In the two holes, he fixed two three-by-three-inch mirrors from his mother's lipstick pouch. He taped one slanting up from the viewing area of each carton. Then he taped the ends of the cartons to each other and painted the periscope green.

"Look, Mom, I have a periscope. With the help of this instrument, submarines can detect ships from the bottom of the ocean," Tommy said excitedly as Carol walked in.

"You're a smart boy. One day you may be an oceanographer."

"No, Mom, I don't like water. I think I'll be an archeologist."

"You'll be dealing with skeletons." She stopped short.

"You were going to tell me something?" Tommy changed the subject.

"Take your insulin shot. Don't forget to floss your teeth; remember, we don't want any new cavities. And do wash your hands with antibacterial soap after you've put Leo to sleep. I'll call at ten to say good night."

"Yes, Mom." Tommy settled down to do his homework.

Neither Carol nor Tommy knew that the next few hours were going to change their lives forever.

CHAPTER 8

After Carol had gone to work, Tommy began his other homework assignments. He had to read about the history of America and give detailed reasons for the population decline of Native Americans. It shrank from an estimated ten million in 1620 to a quarter million in 1850.

He flipped through the pages of the book, highlighting important points. It took him close to an hour to finish the assignment. All the while, Leo was scampering around the room. He did not like it when Tommy worked hard.

Tommy finished his homework, reclined against the chair, closed his eyes, and thought of his father. Today, like every day when he was alone, he missed his father. He remembered playing basketball with him on the porch. Sometimes he would help his father clean the yard and gutters. His father would make hot chocolate, and they would watch an hour of television together.

Tommy's eyes grew moist. He never cried in front of his mother. But alone in the house, where every nook and corner held his dear father's memory, Tommy would be moved to tears.

"I'll never see Dad again." He often repeated those words to himself, and each time they wounded him.

"Dad, I miss you." Tommy held the photograph and lovingly caressed his father's image. His father, after climbing a summit, looked tired but happy. On his lips played the radiant smile of a man who was doing what he loved most: climbing mountains and facing challenges. His deep red hair and equally red stubble reflected the bright sunshine. His blue eyes sparkled with adventure. It was hard to believe that the same love for excitement had taken his life.

"I miss you every day. And don't worry, Dad; I'll take care of Mom." Tommy again touched his father's happy image.

After talking to the picture, he put Leo to bed in his dry aquarium. He then washed up, brushed his teeth, gave himself a shot of insulin, and settled down on the sofa with his dinner. He turned on the TV. There was a horror movie on one channel and a sitcom on Nickelodeon. Carol and Tommy enjoyed watching horror movies together, getting scared, and having a hearty laugh. Normally he did not like to watch horror movies alone, but today he decided to watch *The Haunted House* all by himself. It was a 1950's black-and-white movie. Old movies did not have the punch that could scare an eleven-year-old. However, *The Haunted House* was a classic, and Tommy expected a hundred minutes of wholesome horror while snuggled in his blanket on the sofa.

The movie began with a scene of a dark, dreary graveyard at night. Under a heavy gust of wind and lightening, a tombstone began to move and a skeletal hand appeared from underneath.

"Give me a break! Why can't they be more original?" Tommy yawned.

The moving tombstone on the screen reminded him of young Sean buried beneath that heavy tombstone for over twelve years. *I wonder if Sean had friends and if they played pranks. What were his hobbies? Did he paint?*

Suddenly, the energy in the room changed. Tommy looked up from Sean's grade report and realized that the film had changed to color. There was no haunted house or cemetery in sight; instead, there was a familiar lake and cliffs. There were men arguing with each other in modern clothes. There were recent models of cars and vans parked near the men.

Puzzled, Tommy looked again at the screen, rubbing his eyes. The men on the screen argued and swore at each other. It was definitely not a scene from the movie he had been watching. Tommy turned the volume down, but the sounds only grew louder. He pressed the button to a different channel and was surprised to see the same movie playing on that one too.

He changed it again. It was the same scene on every channel: a bunch of young men arguing and hitting each other above the lake surrounded by rolling mountains. Perplexed, Tommy looked at the remote. *The satellite signal must have gone haywire*, he thought, and turned the TV off. He sighed with relief as silence filled the room.

The next instant, Tommy watched in horror and disbelief as the wall behind the TV lit up, and the same scene played on the white wall, the voices louder this time, as if someone had turned on a movie projector behind Tommy. With a dry mouth and his heart beating like a steam engine, Tommy turned around to see what was projecting the movie. He saw nothing. Behind him was a dark window covered with blinds.

He turned back to the wall with the TV and in that moment realized why it was different. He was seeing Blue Haven Lake, nestled among the rolling cliffs of San Felipe. The men were in a scuffle. The one with broad shoulders and a moustache whipped a knife from his pocket and jabbed the blade into the gut of the shorter, stocky man.

Tommy passed out on the sofa.

CHAPTER 9

"Honey, why did you sleep on the sofa?" Carol asked. "And why was the TV on? I told you to go to bed at ten."

Tommy was surprised to find himself on the sofa under a blanket. He mumbled something about having dozed off last night while watching TV.

"What?" Carol asked.

"I was watching a horror movie and must have fallen asleep." Tommy debated with himself whether he should confide in his mother. In the morning light, he was not even sure what happened last night was real or a reaction to a horror movie. His mother's statement that the TV was on when she came in at dawn confused him.

"Now how can you watch a horror movie without me?" Carol asked playfully. She continued to talk while Tommy got ready for school.

"Next time, remember: only one hour of TV at night after I'm gone. According to new research, the brain goes into neutral when you watch TV. While you passively watch someone else's script, it goes dormant, unless you analyze it, discuss it, or challenge some aspects of the narrative." Carol gave him an excerpt from her brain fitness class.

"Hmm…"Tommy was in deep thought as he quickly ate his cereal.

"Did you hear what I said?" Carol asked.

"Mom, I'm late. I need to go,"Tommy said sullenly. Last night's experience hung heavy on him.

"Are you okay, honey?"

"Yeah."Tommy walked to the door. Then he turned, kissed his mother, and quickly darted out the front door.

"He's missing his father," Carol said to herself.

"Mom, go to sleep, and don't worry about the dishes and vacuuming. I will take care of it when I come back."Tommy gently instructed his mother with the charm she had come to cherish. Then, with those reassuring words, he was gone.

"Ah, that's my boy. He's okay." Carol smiled and looked up to the blue sky and thanked the powers that be who gave her a precious gift in Tommy.

✑

"Now, read from your assignment as to why the Native American population declined from ten million to a quarter million in two hundred years," Ms. Stooksberry instructed the sixth graders. "Megan, you go first."

"The reasons for the decline were"…" Megan began reading.

The class was in progress, and Tommy was deep in thought. What happened yesterday was not a nightmare. He was wide-awake and saw the phenomena. A chill ran down his spine as he remembered the murderous scene moving from the small screen to the wall. What was the meaning of that? Should he tell his counselor? He decided against it. Was it diabetes playing with his nerves? He knew that low blood sugar could trigger a coma, and high blood sugar could cause damage to the nervous system and impair the optical nerves. Did he suffer from hyperglycemia last night? He did not check his blood sugar, but he had his customary insulin injection after a meal.

"Tommy, it's your turn." Ms. Stooksberry's authoritative voice derailed his train of thought.

"The decline in native American population over two hundred years…" Tommy read from the points he had prepared. Everyone listened, because Tommy was a good speaker and history was his strongest subject.

"Well done, Tommy." Ms. Stooksberry was pleased.

***

"Tommy, you're awfully quiet. Is everything all right?" Megan asked Tommy. They were all in the cafeteria for lunch.

"There is something I need to talk about. And please don't think I'm trying to pull your leg, because I'm not," Tommy said thoughtfully.

"What is it, Tommy?" Megan was all attention while Johnny and Pete glanced at each other, not knowing what to expect.

"I had the strangest experience yesterday," Tommy began. "I was watching a horror movie on TV. Suddenly, the old black-and-white movie changed to a color movie where the scene kept repeating. A bunch of rough-looking men were fighting. One of them stabbed the other. It was so graphic that I turned off the TV."

"That *is* the strangest experience." Johnny mocked him.

"It shouldn't be. According to research, by the time American kids are pre-teens, they have watched about eight thousand murders. That, at its best, should have been boring but not the strangest experience." Pete was best at research.

"Go on, Tommy." Megan was her friendly self.

"Well, after I turned off the TV, the scene shifted from the screen to the wall behind the TV set, complete with sound and images. It was as if there was a movie projector behind me facing the wall, but there was nothing. I was totally shocked; I have never been so scared in my life. Even in the cemetery where I was prepared to meet ghosts, I was not scared." Tommy said it all in one breath.

"Then?" asked Pete and Megan.

"Then I passed out on the sofa. I don't remember anything. This morning, my mother woke me up and said that the TV was on," Tommy said with a frown. He knew he was not making any sense.

Megan, Pete, and Johnny stared at Tommy for a few moments.

"Tommy, are you sure you weren't tripping," Megan said.

"C'mon, he's fooling us," Johnny applauded. "For a moment even I was taken in."

"Tommy, we are co-conspirators. We're not the one's you should be playing," Pete said kindly.

Even Megan had a shadow of doubt in her eyes. Tommy made an instant decision. He would have to keep some things close to his heart, or he would lose his friends.

"Oh, fudge. And I thought I could fool you." Tommy laughed loudly. "You guys are one tough lot. Of course I'm kidding."

The friends had a hearty laugh, backslapping each other, except Megan. Something told her that Tommy was telling the truth.

CHAPTER 10

T ommy's mind was a jumble of thoughts and images. He still had vivid memories of the night when TV scenes transferred to the wall. His friends did not believe him. Megan looked like she wanted to, but the incident was so incredible that she was afraid to support him openly. Tommy decided he would not dwell on that experience. He also decided not to tell his mother. She would think something was wrong with him and take him for counseling or psychiatric evaluation. Everyone would blame it on diabetes.

It was evening, and the breeze was turning cool. Tommy watched from the dining room table, as his mother got ready to go to the hospital. She left for work after giving him the usual instructions. He looked at the clock, checked his blood sugar, and then gave himself a shot of insulin. He ate pasta and meatballs from the fridge without heating the food. He fed Leo bits of pasta with his mealworms. When Carol called at nine to go over the checklist, he told her he was tired and planned to go to sleep early.

With that out of the way, he put on his jacket and put Leo snugly in his pocket. From the garage, he picked up the flashlight and checked the batteries. He then rode his bike to Pete's house. They were all going to meet at the cemetery.

Tommy stopped under Pete's bedroom, took out a tennis ball from his back-pack, and gently threw the ball at Pete's second-story bedroom window and waited. The window slid open and Pete looked out. He whispered loudly.

"I can't go. Mom needs help sorting her files. Sorry," Pete said.

"Okay, I'll go with Johnny and Megan," Tommy said with a touch of disap-pointment. "Johnny's father wants him and Megan to clean the attic." With that Pete quickly slid the window shut.

That threw a wrench in the plan. Tommy was disappointed. He had a whole evening to himself, and he was done for the day; even his homework was fin-ished. Slowly he cycled back to his house. The cemetery was on the way, and it looked eerie in the light of the waning moon and myriads of stars scattered in the sky. He trembled for a moment at the thought that a boy his age, with whom he shared a birthday, was buried there. It was a life cut short by tragedy. And in a bizarre, random prank, Tommy was chosen to play that boy. The research on Sean Butler and the accident in which the whole family perished made Tommy feel empathy for Sean.

With these thoughts assailing him, Tommy wanted to get away from the cemetery. Just then, Leo, who was dozing in his pocket, sprang out and dashed to the gate of the cemetery.

"Leo, come back. It's too dark. We can't play now," Tommy called out, switching on his flashlight. But Leo made the chittering sound that he made when excited and disappeared in the desolate darkness. Tommy cursed under his breath. Leo needed a time out, but for now, Tommy just had to find him. He parked his bike against the gate, crept underneath the fence, and ran after Leo. He followed the familiar sound of his gecko. Finally he saw his pet standing on a headstone, wiping his eyeballs with his long, snakelike tongue.

"C'mon, Leo, let's go. I don't want to be here all alone." Tommy slowly moved toward Leo, but the stubborn reptile, enjoying his antics, slipped out of Tommy's reach.

Gently, Tommy reached out, grabbed Leo's belly, and put him in his pocket. He was about to turn and leave when he saw the name on the gravestone: Sean Butler. Tommy stared at it in silent wonder.

Any normal day, Tommy would have been scared of being alone in the cemetery at nightfall without a living soul. What if he met a couple of ghosts? Was he prepared? Tommy stood there a few minutes in silence. When he did walk away, it was with a feeling of affinity with the Butler family, especially Sean.

It was lunchtime, and the school cafeteria was teeming with hungry students. Tommy looked out the window at the dark clouds that covered the sun. Megan, Pete, and Johnny brought their trays to his table. Tommy looked thoughtful.

"You're awfully quiet today," Megan said.

Tommy did not hear her. Since that night when he drew the pencil that chose him to play Sean Butler, Tommy had started to feel estranged from his surroundings. His feelings were muddled. His friends were cross at the thought of Tommy playing a prank on them. Megan was kind and gentle, but then she had a brother who was a bully of sorts.

As the trio placed their lunch trays on the table, a few students moved away from them. This group included the two students Johnny had talked into buying them chocolate sundaes.

"What's your problem?" demanded Johnny indignantly. Before they could respond, the bespectacled O'Flaherty sisters approached the table.

The nerdy Sarah and Clara O'Flaherty pretended to be identical twins, even though they were born a year apart. They wore similar clothes, sported the same-length ponytails, and both wore eyeglasses even though only one needed prescription glasses. They even tried to get similar grades. When one would get a low grade, the other managed the same. When one got sick, the other stayed home in sympathy.

"Tommy, how many synonyms are there for weird?" Sarah and Clara asked in unison.

"He's not weird." A boy at the other table giggled.

"Yeah, it takes guts to be weird." Another kid chuckled.

"Let's play reincarnation of Sean Butler," a girl nearby said with a straight face.

"Yeah! Let's roast marshmallows at the cemetery and see if we can meet some interesting ghosts," said another.

"And if the ghosts try to act funny, I'll shoot them with my BB gun," another boy said, mimicking Johnny's deep voice. Everyone around their table burst out laughing.

The Furtive Four looked miffed as they watched their meticulously planned arrangement unravel. Johnny was quick to make sense of it all.

"You coward! You snitched on us," Johnny barked in Pete's face.

Instinctively, Tommy and Johnny knew that Pete had decided to blow their plan because he did not like going to the cemetery. Johnny grabbed Pete's collar.

"He's not Sean Butler." Pete tried to get his collar out of Johnny's grip

"He *is* Sean Butler," Johnny said with authority.

"Let him go, Johnny. You're such a bully." Megan knew that Pete was not comfortable with their prank.

"I don't like going to the cemetery." Pete finally disentangled himself from Johnny's menacing grip. Silence filled the cafeteria.

"It's okay, Johnny. We should respect his views," Tommy said gently.

"He spilled the beans. He has to pay for it." Johnny was looking for trouble.

"Wait a minute. What's all the fuss about? I am Sean Butler," Tommy said.

"Shut up. You're not Sean Butler," Johnny growled.

"That's what I mean. He's not," Pete said.

"Shut up. He is Sean Butler." Johnny was beginning to get confused.

"That's what I said. I am Sean Butler," Tommy repeated without emotion.

"What do you mean you're Sean?" Johnny peered into Tommy's face.

"I *am* the reincarnation of Sean Butler." Even though Tommy said it flatly, his voice resonated in the quiet cafeteria. Johnny looked with killer intent toward Tommy, who had the attention of half the school; the other half would be informed by the time school was over.

"Are you trying to pull our leg?" Megan looked hurt.

"So you think you're Superman, pretending to be someone's ghost and behaving like a hero?" Johnny finally said what was bothering him.

"I'm not pretending. I *am* Sean Butler reincarnated as Thomas Stevenson. It was not just a coincidence that we started playing this prank. I have not been the same since. There are strange things happening to me. I can't explain them, but I do believe that I am Sean," Tommy said loudly. Some students snickered while others watched in silence, a couple of teachers exchanged glances.

"You were randomly selected to play Sean Butler," Megan said softly. "Anyone could have been Sean."

"I know, Megan. I know. But how do you explain what happened with my TV that night? Yesterday I was returning from Pete's house, and Leo jumped out and ran inside the cemetery. I chased him, and he went straight for Sean's grave." Tommy was out of breath.

"I'm not afraid," Pete said, looking pale.

"And what evidence do you have of those two incidents happening to you?" Johnny asked, voicing the disbelief of everyone in the room.

"I can swear on my dead father that I am telling the truth…"

"Oh shut up! You're not Tommy the reincarnate but Tommy the liar. We wanted to be funny, but you turned us into freaks." With that, Johnny collected his tray and moved to another table. Pete and Megan followed Johnny, he more eagerly than her. The three-year relationship of the Furtive Four had ended abruptly.

CHAPTER 11

"Ms. Stooksberry, I'm not going to give credence to wagging tongues," the principal retorted. "Tommy is creative. You often told me that he comes up with the most original ideas."

"He's good at studies, especially history and social studies, and he always does extra research. However, this time he has gone too far. I think he seriously believes he is Sean Butler born again. I think this is more than a practical joke. Even his closest friends are not talking to him," Ms. Stooksberry pleaded.

"Yes, but you have often talked about Tommy's narrative skills and the fact that the boy could produce a story out of thin air and tell it like it was real." The principal put a stop to any further rumors about Tommy.

The whole school was abuzz with the breakup of the prankster group. Everyone avoided Tommy as if he had a contagious disease.

Tommy needed his friends, but they had become adversaries. No one was willing to show empathy for the dramatic changes taking place in his life. He looked thoughtful most of the time. He was not creating trouble, but he was also not paying attention in class. However, being a good student, he completed his assignments and continued to maintain good grades.

The news of Tommy Stevenson, self-declared reincarnation of Sean Butler, spread from the school to the residents of San Felipe. The only person who was completely oblivious to what was brewing under her own roof was Tommy's mother. The middle school principal was also unaware until sources outside the confines of the school confronted him with news of the phenomenon.

⌀

The principal was taken by surprise when he received a call from Derek Spalding, a reporter from *The Daily Post*, about Tommy Stevenson's assertion of reincarnation.

"No, sir, you may not," the irate principal said to the nosey reporter who wanted to interview Tommy. "This is a respectable school and so far untainted by any gobbledygook. It is the policy of this school to admit students who have one, and I repeat *one*, bona fide birth certificate."

"Sir, I need only ten minutes with Tommy to confirm that it is indeed gobbledygook. I'm on your side," said Derek Spalding.

"Mr. Spalding, which part of *no* don't you understand!" the principal said and slammed the phone.

In the *Daily Post* newspaper office, Matt, Spalding's colleague, smiled as he saw the green light on the telephone stopped blinking. Spalding, however, pretended to continue talking with the principal who was not there.

"Yes, sir, ten minutes only. Thank you, and have a good day, sir," he said into a dead phone.

"Hey, Matt, cover for me, will you? Tell the fat man I'm chasing a story," Spalding said, pointing to the editor's office.

"You don't stand a ghost of a chance," said Matt and smiled knowingly as he watched Spalding put on his jacket and print out directions to Thurgood Marshall Elementary School. "Whatever I say, he's going to think you're in a singles bar picking up a new divorcee," Matt hollered after him, but Spalding was already gone.

Derek Spalding, a reporter at large, was brilliant when it came to sniffing a story and unraveling it in atypical manner. He was fiercely private, independent, and suspicious of everyone, especially women. He believed that a UFO was less complicated than an ordinary woman. His colleagues called him a nonconforming misogynist since he had married and divorced the same woman twice. As his ambition to host the respected Sunday TV magazine show slowly took over his persona, so did his addiction to alcohol and investigative reporting.

Spalding had earned fame and respect when he cracked the case of the murder of an elderly man living on a secluded hill. The police claimed they were close to nailing the murderer. However, Spalding beat them to it and earned peer respect, media attention, and a raise. He was so happy that he drank himself into the hospital.

❧

School was over for the day. The exit gate was crowded as students were leaving. Tommy looked at his friends Johnny, Pete, and Megan going into the parking lot. He missed them. He wanted them to trust him, but it seemed like a remote possibility. He could see Megan sending him a friendly look, but she could not go against the others in the group. Tommy could see that she was torn. She knew that Tommy would not lie to her, yet her rational mind was not willing to accept his incredulous story.

"Pete, Megan, can I talk to you?" Tommy said as they passed by him, but Johnny blocked his way.

"Hello." A young man in his late thirties, wearing a crumpled light-gray raincoat walked up to Tommy as the young boy stood sulking in the parking space. "I'm Derek Spalding, reporter from the *Daily Post*. I have come especially to talk to you."

"Sorry, I don't talk to strangers," Tommy said flatly.

"I won't be a stranger for long." Spalding produced a business card from his jacket. "I heard about your incredible story and wanted to talk to you."

Tommy looked the other way. He needed friends, not a grown-up stranger.

"I believe your story. I don't think you are kidding," Spalding said reassuringly.

Tommy did not respond. He began to walk away from the man who smelled of alcohol.

"I have something for you." With that, Spalding produced a printout from the George Washington Elementary School 1995 yearbook. Tommy stared at the photo of Sean Butler. He hesitated for a moment. His friends were not talking to him, and he desperately wanted to communicate with someone about his experience. Leo gave a chirpy call from the inner pocket of Tommy's shirt and poked his head out. Spalding was startled as Leo stood on Tommy's shoulders, cleaned his eyes with his tongue, and stared at the reporter.

"Mary, mother of Jesus, what a surprise. It's a leopard gecko, if I'm not mistaken. You must tell me about this creature. I too need a friend who will keep me company and guard my wallet. Is it a male?" asked Spalding.

"Yes, his name is Leo," Tommy replied eagerly.

"I should get a female gecko, and if they become friends, then maybe we too can be friends. What would I call her?" Spalding had found an opening.

"You could call her Kizzy. That's what I was planning to name the female gecko that my father promised to bring back from his climbing expedition," Tommy said in one breath. He was beginning to like the reporter. Anyone he could talk to about his father and Leo would be his friend.

"Where's your father?" Spalding asked walking past the school gate.

"That's a long story," Tommy said, walking in step with the reporter.

"And I have all the time in the world." Spalding pointed at a bench in the park across from the school.

CHAPTER 12

"My dad loved to go on climbing expeditions. He used to take groups of climbers on expeditions, especially to the Himalayas. But on the last trip, a massive earthquake destroyed the whole region in northern Pakistan, and I lost him." Tommy continued to tell Spalding of the aftermath of the earthquake. "The valley where Dad and the party of climbers were resting disappeared completely. And to this day we have never recovered the bodies."

"I'm truly sorry," Spalding said sadly.

It was getting chilly, and they had been talking for an hour at the Giant Burger. It was time for both to leave. Throughout the conversation, Spalding was all attention and diligently took notes. Tommy narrated the incident at the cemetery. "I was randomly chosen to play the reincarnation of Sean Butler. It was all fun and games. I soon found out that Sean Butler and I share the same birthday. That was a weird coincidence."

"Then?"

"Then things started to happen. I don't feel the same, and my friends don't believe me. They are angry. They think I'm seeking attention." Spalding listened attentively. He could not believe his luck. He had stumbled upon a great story. Even though he did not give it much credibility, it would make great copy.

"Before the trip to the cemetery, you never…?" Spalding was mesmerized.

"No, everything started to happen after that day at the cemetery."

"So are these thoughts, ideas or…?"

"Images, like on the TV screen. How the movie started to play on the wall. There was the dead bee in the vase, the grave with Sean's name, and the incident in the school swimming pool. I really felt I was going to drown even though my friends thought I was acting."

"Tommy, I believe everything you told me." Spalding patted his shoulder gently. "We've been together for two hours already. I hope I'm not a stranger now. Are we friends?"

"I guess." Tommy shook hands with him. "Do you own a gun? I've never seen a real gun."

Spalding ignored Tommy's question. "Here's my cell phone number. I'm available 24/7. Promise you'll call me when you need to talk and you'll not talk to anyone else about your experience. The world is full of byline burglars," he said, producing a small digital camera from his pocket.

"You don't mind?"

"For the newspaper? All right," Tommy said excitedly.

❧❧

Dawn was breaking; Carol looked tired, but she was happy to get away from the hospital. She was glad to have the next two days off from work. She changed her clothes and went to the front desk to sign off for the night. She was immediately aware of an uneasy silence around her.

"What?" she asked her colleagues around the reception desk. They remained quiet. She followed their gaze to the newspaper on the counter. Carol was stunned to find Tommy's picture on the front page of a local newspaper along with a photo of another boy called Sean Butler. She quickly read the headline.

Tommy Twiceborn
Reincarnation Or Prank

"Has something terrible happened to Tommy?" she asked hysterically and rushed out before anyone could respond. She drove home at breakneck speed, almost running a red light. Before anyone could explain that it was not a life-threatening situation, Carol had reached home. Breathless with anxiety, yet relieved to see him okay, she stood before her son with a newspaper in her hand.

"Why do I have to read about you in the newspaper? Do you know what that does to me? Where did you learn about reincarnation?" Carol asked all her questions at once.

"Mom, let me explain!"

"Tommy, I get enough spooky stuff at work with people who are sick or who think they are sick; I don't need to be spooked at home. Who is Derek Spalding?" She waved the newspaper in Tommy's face.

Tommy stayed quiet. He was excited to have his photo in the newspaper but had not anticipated the consequences.

"I want the phone number of that reporter you talked to without my permission," Carol yelled.

"Mom, it was my decision to talk to him."

"Your decision to talk to a stranger!" Carol yelled so loud that she began to choke. "You're an eleven-year-old. I can have him arrested for stalking you, for getting all the information from you about us." She was beside herself with anxiety and exasperation. She reached out, pulled a business card from Tommy's shirt pocket, and quickly dialed the number.

"Good morning, this is the *Daily Post*. How may I direct your call?" said the person who answered.

"Straight to the editor," Carol said brusquely.

"And who should I say is calling?" the receptionist asked politely.

"Tomorrow's news."

"Yes, ma'am," the receptionist said calmly. "May I take your phone number, and I'll have him call you. What is it about?"

Frustrated, Carol hung up and turned angrily to Tommy, waving the newspaper in his face. "I don't want to read about you in the newspaper. I read about your father in the same newspaper. And that was the last I heard of him."

Next day, Carol Stevenson called the editor, Goldstein, again and threatened to sue the newspaper for violating their privacy.

"Okay, okay," Goldstein said. "Next time we'll get your permission before talking to Tommy."

Carol continued her tirade for several moments and then hung up angrily.

"Spalding!" Goldstein opened the door of his office and thundered above the din of the workers. "I want you in here ASAP."

Spalding entered, smiling. The editor was in a foul mood. That usually meant they were going to have a row, and that would give Spalding a chance to walk out angrily and get himself a drink across the street. He had told the editor if he got mad at work, he would drink at work.

"You met the boy outside the school? Tommy's mother will sue us!" the editor thundered at Spalding.

"A favorite American pastime." Spalding yawned.

"I told you to follow up on the tax evasion story concerning Schroeder and Schroeder."

"Tax evasion, road rage, drunk drivers, bearded terrorists, unnecessary wars. Every goddamn reporter in the country is recycling the same garbage," Spalding retorted angrily.

"You'll do as I tell you," Goldstein barked back as the phone rang. He picked up the phone and listened. "Yeah…is that right? Okay, keep me posted. Thank you." He hung up the phone looking mellow, almost friendly. "Okay, you may go," he said with an uncharacteristic smile.

"What?" Spalding was puzzled. He paused for a minute, and then it struck him. "It's sold out, isn't it? The edition with Tommy's story."

"We broke the story. Now go follow up," Goldstein said in a low voice.

"What do you mean, 'we'? Unless you're the mouse in my pocket."

"Get out and do some work." The editor smiled.

"*I* broke the story, and *I'll* follow up. Nobody says 'we' when I'm on the beat," Spalding said arrogantly before he exited.

"Everyone's invited to the bar. It's on me," Spalding announced to his coworkers like a man who had won a match uncontested.

"Mrs. Stevenson, I apologize profusely for my lapse. I should've talked to you first." Spalding, a picture of humility, stood in Carol's living room like a man condemned.

"I hope you're genuinely sorry. Please sit down. You're making me nervous," Carol said disdainfully while Tommy looked at her with anxiety. It was an uneasy moment for all three. Carol was about to say something when she noticed Tommy looking anxious. She could see he liked the reporter and needed a male figure in his life, but she was not sure if Spalding was the right influence for her son, even temporarily. She was also coming to grips with the fact that even if it were not Spalding, some other reporter or neighbor would be bothering them. Her son had become the talk of the town in a matter of weeks, and the situation was irreversible.

"Okay, but remember, if you jeopardize his safety in any way, that will be the end of this privilege. I will make sure you will never get a byline in any newspaper." She said brusquely.

"That's fair. I also promise to protect him against media mongers," Spalding said with relief.

Tommy smiled with satisfaction. He had convinced his mother not to press charges against the reporter.

CHAPTER 13

"Okay, honey, check your blood sugar and take your insulin." Carol was calling from the hospital. It was nine o'clock, and she had taken a break to talk to Tommy.

"Okay, Mom, I have taken the insulin and am going to have dinner. Good night."

"Good night, honey, and one hour of TV only."

Tommy settled down on the sofa with his dinner plate. He had finished his homework and had done all the chores his mother had asked him to do. He was going to watch one hour of a cowboy movie.

Ten minutes into the movie, there was a scene where a few cowboys were having a drunken brawl among the rugged mountains. One man got angry, took out his lasso, and strangled another man. Tommy had seen many such scenes, but in that moment, he felt a chilling sensation in his stomach and the food tasted like acid in his mouth. He stared at the screen and stopped eating. He reached for his glass of milk and looked up again; the man being strangled was slowly going blue in the face. Tommy choked as he quickly gulped the milk, his eyes glued to the screen. The lifeless body of the strangled man dangled in the hands of the killer and then fell to the ground.

Suddenly, Tommy felt bile in his mouth. He rushed to the bathroom and, holding the toilet bowl in both arms, threw up. He then returned to the living room and turned off the TV. As he snuggled under the blanket, he thought about the scene. Like any eleven-year-old American boy, he must have seen seven or eight thousand murders on TV, but he had never had that reaction before.

❧

"Come on, honey. It's getting late," Carol called from the living room. It was her day off, and she was going to drive Tommy to school. Just when they got into the car and she grabbed the wheel, her restless son said, "Sorry, Mom, I need to go to the restroom." Tommy stepped out of the car and darted into the house. Once inside, he quickly dialed Spalding's number.

"Who's this in the middle of the night?" said a very drunk man on the other end of the phone.

"It's eight in the morning, Mr. Spalding. There is something I urgently have to tell you: I don't think Sean died of drowning," Tommy said, looking anxiously at his mother through the kitchen window.

"Who's Sean?" Spalding's words were slurred. He was totally sloshed.

"The boy in the cemetery. I want to talk to you." Tommy was miffed at Spalding. "Can we meet at recess?"

"Maybe after school."

"After school I have baseball practice."

"After baseball practice."

"After baseball I have to go with Mom to a pie competition. It's a fund-raiser for after-school programs."

"C'mon, honey, we don't want to be late," Carol hollered from the car.

"I must go now," Tommy said quickly.

"Tomorrow. We'll meet tomorrow then." Spalding wanted to get off the phone and nurse his hangover. "And remember, mum's the word."

Tommy was irritated. If only that reporter was less drunk, he would be more alert. Tommy desperately needed to talk to someone. All night, the image of the strangled man haunted him, and he kept breaking into a sweat. After tossing and turning in bed, the dots began to connect and a horrifying picture had emerged.

During baseball practice, Tommy was still thinking about the movie when he had a mishap. The ball came at him at high speed. He tried to catch it, and it hit his right index finger hard. The pain blinded him. Within minutes, his finger had swollen and turned red. Carol, who was watching his practice with other parents, knew right away her son had a minor fracture and needed help.

They rushed to the hospital where the x-ray showed a hairline fracture. An hour later, they came out of the hospital, and Tommy had a cast from his finger to the forearm.

"Let's go home."

"No, Mom, I don't want you to miss the pie competition. Let's go."

Carol smiled as they drove to the event just in time for the final awards presentation. There were many people, and photographers were taking pictures.

A reporter approached Tommy, smiling. "May I take your photo, Tommy? And maybe we can talk a little."

"Are you a friend of Spalding?" Tommy asked innocently.

"Of course. We know each other very well." The reporter clicked a shot. "How about if we talk a bit?"

"Sure, a friend of Spalding is also a friend of mine."

An unshaven Spalding entered the large newspaper office. His shirt and pants looked crumpled and slept in. He had not brushed his hair. A female copy editor he passed covered her nose gracefully. There was silence in the hall as he moved to his desk. The sudden quiet in the hall meant trouble.

"I smell rebellion in the air. Or is it just a robust hangover?" said Spalding, sniffing the air.

"The fat man wants you," Matt said softly.

"Okay, I can take it on the chin now that I'm appropriately wasted," Spalding got up from his chair. Scratching his two-day stubble, he staggered to the editor's room.

Everyone in the hall waited, motionless, staring at the large golden plaque outside the editor's door. It said, "Rule number 1: the boss is always right. Rule number 2: refer to Rule number 1." As Spalding shut the door behind him, thunderous yelling shattered the silence. With the tension in the hall dissipated, everything returned to normal in the newsroom.

Matt looked at the fresh edition of their rival newspaper, *Midday Journal*. It had Tommy's picture on the front page and a screaming headline.

Reincarnated Tommy Claims Sean Was Murdered

Inside the editor's office, visibly embarrassed, Spalding faced the fury of Goldstein, who pushed a copy of the rival newspaper in the reporter's face.

"I told you to stay close. Close to the story, not to the bottle," the editor roared. "I will not be shafted by an inept reporter and an almost-bankrupt *Midday Journal.*"

A surprised Spalding began to read the story.

"You haven't even read the story? And you want to anchor a TV news show!" The editor was further outraged.

"I told him not to talk to anyone," Spalding said feebly. He wanted to kick himself.

"You told an eleven-year-old not to tell anyone the most exciting discovery of his life. Someone *smarter* and *sober* got the better of you, and we are left with egg on our face." The editor looked like he was about to tear out his hair.

"I'm sorry. Give me a break. It won't happen again." All the euphoria of the previous week's celebration ebbed out of his body. Sullenly, Spalding turned around to leave the room.

"Wait." The editor stopped Spalding and said into the intercom. "Send her in."

Next moment, a blonde woman in her late thirties or early forties entered, looking intimidated. *Now what is the fat man up to?* Spalding's mind began to race.

"This is Moira Shaughnessy. Moira, meet Derek Spalding, one of our finest reporters, also known as Mr. Hubris by his colleagues." He then turned to Spalding and said, "She joined us today. She is your partner."

"Mary, mother of Jesus! Where's she from, *Candid Camera* or *Death Squad?* I don't like working with anyone, least of all women. They're trouble."

Spalding did not get a good feeling about Moira, but suffering from his hangover, he did not have a good feeling about anything. Moira looked cautious and diligent, as if she did not have the guts to be spontaneous. She watched nervously as the two men argued over her.

"You'll do as you're told. This story is getting complex. I want you two to stay on top of it. If you screw up again, I'll make sure you never get your byline in any newspaper again. And you can forget about hosting the Sunday television show." With that warning, the editor picked up the telephone, a sign that he wanted to be alone.

Embarrassed, Spalding walked out. Moira and he had started on the wrong foot already.

"So you're hired to keep an eye on me, *Partner?*" Spalding decided to show his acerbic side right away.

"Look, I'm a rookie, but I'm detail-oriented. I was doing research at the *Midday Journal*, but they're going to fold," Moira said humbly.

"Aha! *Midday Journal.* The perfect mole of an imperfect newspaper. How much are they paying you for spying on me?" Spalding had decided to bully her from the start.

"They can't even pay me to make coffee. By the way, I make good coffee."

Spalding paused for a moment; he knew he was stuck with her. She did not look assertive, and she could do research for him.

"Let's go talk to Tommy. You know about the boy?"

"I'm fascinated by that story. I would love to meet him."

They got into Spalding's old Buick and drove off. They did not notice a black Volkswagen Beetle that was following them.

CHAPTER 14

"Christ!" Spalding blurted with exasperation as he saw a police car parked outside Tommy's house.

He was still reeling under the impact of everything that had happened since morning. The hangover was getting worse.

Tommy came running to him as Spalding parked in the driveway.

"Tommy, this is my assistant Moira; she'll be working with me. She also makes good coffee." Spalding wanted to lay the parameters of their relationship right away.

"Hi Moira." He turned to Spalding. "I'm sorry. The photographer at the pie competition said you sent him to talk to me. He lied to me."

"What happened?" Spalding pointed at Tommy's bandaged finger, ignoring his apology.

"Hairline fracture. I was playing baseball, and the ball hit my finger."

Petrocelli, the pot-bellied inspector, walked over to them. He had a big, ruddy face and dark brown eyes with a receding hairline. He had been on the police force for over twenty years and was close to retiring. He frowned as he saw Spalding step out of the car. They confronted each other like gladiators with their weapons drawn: the inspector armed with his baton and the reporter with a pen.

"Hi, snoopy. What do you want?" Inspector Petrocelli asked gruffly.

"Just doing my job, Inspector Pasta," Spalding said, looking at the officer's potbelly. Petrocelli was Italian, and Spalding could never resist the temptation to take a dig at him.

"The inspector came to see me." Tommy sensed the tension between the two and intervened. "He was in charge of the Butler family case twelve years ago."

There was a moment of silence when all three understood the implications of those words.

"So you were in charge of the Butler family murder investigation twelve years ago?" Spalding eyed Inspector Petrocelli critically.

"Murder my foot. The Butler family died of drowning. I was the one who ordered the search of the missing family. And I was the one present when the bodies of Philip and Mary Butler were pulled out. It was on my beat that Sean Butler's body was discovered downstream a week later," Petrocelli said with a measure of pride.

"And you were so busy eating meatballs that you forgot to order the autopsies and buried them quickly." Spalding had done his homework.

"Well, we're a small town. The loss of an entire family was a big tragedy, so we ordered a quick and decent burial. Besides, there was no foul play, and we hold that opinion even now." The inspector had turned red.

"And what are you doing here?"

"Just came to check out the claim of a boy who says he is the reincarnation of Sean Butler, the boy I saw buried twelve years ago. I think this past life mumbo jumbo is a cock-and-bull story. Whatever happened to real news?" the inspector said. "What are you doing here?"

"I'm here for the same reason, curiosity and love of adventure." Spalding looked around.

"Adventure, for a man who married the same woman twice? You should be investigating yourself." Petrocelli laughed loudly as he got into his car.

Spalding could have punched the inspector but his cell phone rang.

Moira turned to Tommy and smiled. "How do you feel about this whole reincarnation business?"

"That trip to the cemetery to meet ghosts changed my life." Tommy excitedly told her what happened at the cemetery. "I want this to end soon so I can have my friends back."

For several moments, Moira silently stared at the overcast sky.

"Tommy, I'm absolutely captivated by your story," she began softly. "Today is my first day as a reporter, and I never expected to hear the most sensational story of my life." Her blue eyes locked with his. "Are we friends?"

"Cool, of course we are. And you must say hello to my friend Leo," Tommy said.

"Where is your friend?" Moira looked around.

"Leo," Tommy called out, and the gecko sprang out of Tommy's shirt pocket and perched himself on Tommy's shoulder extended his tongue, and wiped his large, green eyes.

"Do you like him?"

"Of course!" Startled, Moira stepped back.

∽⧓∾

A young boy with glasses played baseball in the schoolyard. He looked up at the dark, menacing clouds gathering strength. A downpour seemed imminent. The boy wanted to go home and be with his parents, but his friends wanted him to play baseball. It began to drizzle. The batter hit the ball with a fury. The boy in the outfield caught the ball in his grip, but the speed with which the ball came made him stagger. As he fell back, he heard a crack, like a branch.

The sky grew darker. The boy looked up at the clouds that seemed to descend on the schoolyard. His playmates disappeared behind the clouds. Their voices echoed to him through a darkened tunnel. The echo turned into a crescendo of loud sounds, urging him to go on playing. He tried to stand but fell again on the muddy ground as the drizzle turned into a downpour.

The boy looked up at the tree and saw a branch was about to break loose. He felt a wave of pain and looked at his index finger. It was hanging loose on his hand. With pain and horror, he began to faint as he heard noises that grew shrill.

"Sean!" A dozen anxious faces surrounded him.

Sweating and gasping for breath, Tommy woke up from his nightmare. He looked at the clock. It was 3:00 a.m. and dark in the room except for the little Snoopy night-light. For several moments, he stared at his bandaged finger before he fell back to sleep.

∽⧓∾

It was Sunday morning, and Tommy was up early, still reeling under the impact of last night's dream. He tried to play video games but could not concentrate. He was convinced someone or something was trying to give him a hint. Thoughts and images, dreams and events crashed in his brain like giant waves on a stormy ocean. He needed answers, but at that moment, he had none.

"Honey, you want to go to church today?" Carol called out. They had started to attend church after the tragedy took Frank away.

"Yes, Mom, I'd love to," Tommy replied, even though he did not want to go anywhere.

However, once at the service, Tommy was glad to be there. He loved the old, redbrick Georgian church with a gabled entrance and an impressive wood-carved pulpit. Sunlight filtered through the stained glass, and a peaceful ambiance lifted his mood as he watched others sing in unison. He shut his eyes and savored the serenity. In that moment, he imagined a golden umbrella descend on him from the blue sky, engulfing his entire being. Something mysterious bathed him in a feeling of protective warmth. He felt perfectly safe in that moment, and a thought dawned on him. *There is a reason why strange things are happening to me. I must not be frightened.* He also needed to speak to Spalding as soon as possible and get the latest incredible revelation off his chest.

Later that evening when his mom was in the kitchen preparing dinner, Tommy phoned Spalding.

"I have something to tell you," Tommy said hurriedly. "When Sean died, he had a fractured finger."

"Are you sure?"

"Of course not, but I had a dream."

"It's only a dream."

"Yes, it's only a dream." Tommy hung up just as his mom called him for dinner.

CHAPTER 15

The newspaper office was feverishly busy. The noise of dozens of keyboards filled the room. The deadline for printing was approaching. There was a flurry of interaction amid copy editors, reporters, layout artists, and photographers.

"How do you spell your name?" Spalding was at Moira's desk.

"Here, I'm Irish," Moira said as she held the nameplate from her desk. It read Moira Allen Shaughnessy.

"Irish, how would you spell 'potato famine'?" Spalding asked with a smirk.

"The same way you'd spell English pomposity," Moira replied acidly, "with a capital *P*." Spalding sighed and moved away from her table. He liked feisty women, but not at work.

"Are we going to meet with Tommy today?" Moira asked.

"I've already met him. I'm preparing the report."

"Why didn't you take me with you?"

"I took my laptop."

"The editor said we should both—"

"When I do a story, I'm the boss." Spalding cut her short. "Besides, after talking with him today, I have a roaring scoop strong enough to knock down the leaning tower of Pisa," he said with a mischievous grin.

"I take it you are talking about Inspector Petrocelli," Moira said flatly. She continued to pound on her keyboard and looked at Spalding out of the corner of her eye. "You're not the dumb blonde I thought you were."

Alone in his cubicle, Spalding reclined on his chair and twiddled his thumbs. It was something he did only after making a bold decision.

After talking to Tommy, Spalding had concluded that he must keep Tommy's story on the front burner. Every day he was inching toward his goal of hosting the Sunday TV show.

He reflected on Tommy's newest revelation in the bizarre case of possible reincarnation. Tommy had told Spalding that when Sean died, he possibly had a hairline fracture in his right index finger. The shadowy images from his dream had convinced Tommy of the same. It was a long shot. Spalding had taken the editor into confidence. Should he break that piece of information or leave it aside? He was testing the resilience of the sleepy town of San Felipe. The story had already put the town in the headlines.

Spalding muddled through his thoughts. What if he, along with the newspaper, was proved wrong? They would lose face, as the editor said. Then again, no one had a story like this, and the sales had shot through the roof.

"God help me!" Spalding, a self-declared agnostic, looked to the ceiling.

In the next few days, Spalding started to read on the fascinating subject of reincarnation and was astonished to find that nearly three thousand cases of reincarnation had been recorded and investigated worldwide. More than two hundred cases have been validated in the twentieth century.

Children, sometimes as young as two years old, who would speak of things and events they would be too young to know, recounted most of the past-life recollections. Some kids spoke of complicated pregnancies, flying fighter planes, experiencing the trauma of war, blood, death, and so forth.

The phone rang. It was Tommy.

"I have to tell you this interesting story of reincarnation from India. I also have pictures and the video of an interview of this woman who remembered her past life," Tommy said excitedly.

"Good. Let's meet today at the Giant Burger," Spalding said.

❦

It was a sunny but slightly chilly afternoon. It was early autumn, and the days were beginning to get shorter. Spalding and Moira met Tommy in the Giant Burger eatery. It was warm, and the sound of burgers sizzling over charcoal was appetizing.

Before they ordered, Tommy took out his glucose meter and tested his blood. The meter showed a reading of 140 mm.

"It's slightly high. I'm going to avoid French fries today. I'd like to order a fish filet with tossed salad," Tommy said.

"Tommy, I'm impressed," Moira said genuinely.

"Thank you. Kids with type one diabetes have to be responsible and alert."

With that out of the way, Tommy began to read from a paper about the fascinating tale of an eight-year-old girl in India.

"In 1926, Shanti Devi was born in a middle-class household in the capital, New Delhi. She was an ordinary child until, at the tender age of three, she amused her family by talking of her husband and sons. The parents concluded that their three-year-old was going to marry early and began to collect her dowry. As the years rolled by, Shanti Devi spoke of a husband and sons so often and with such clarity that the alarmed parents decided to have her examined by the family physician.

"Shanti Devi told the physician that she was talking about a previous lifetime in which her name was Lugdi. In her previous life, she was happily married to a young man named Kedarnath, in a town called Mathura, about two hundred miles from where she was presently living. She said that she had died in 1925 of a complicated pregnancy and described the procedure in such detail that it left the doctor and her parents stunned.

"Shanti Devi, who was six years old at the time, gave details of her hometown, Mathura, where she had lived in her previous life. She remembered her husband, her in-laws, and even the structure of the house. She also recalled that her maternal family lived close to her husband's house.

"Her present family began to investigate her claims, and to their surprise, they found a man by the same name at that address whose wife had died in childbirth several years ago. He had remarried since, and his eldest son was in his twenties.

"The father and son were contacted and persuaded to visit Shanti Devi's home in the neighboring city since the eight-year-old girl insisted on seeing her husband and son. The puzzled father and son came unannounced to Shanti Devi's house. Instantly the little girl recognized them and hugged the man and his twenty-year-old son. She then began to recount events from her past life to her astounded husband. He was especially stunned when she reminded him of an intimate conversation she had with him as his wife.

"You had promised me that if I were to die, you would never remarry for the sake of our sons," she reprimanded him.

Tommy paused and continued. "It was then that the man was convinced that the eight-year-old was indeed his wife from the past. She narrated many events and conversations they had had during their married life. She then expressed her desire to revisit the house in which they had lived as husband and wife where he now lived with his new wife and children. Awed and confused, father and son, unable to cope with that revelation, slipped back into their town.

"The event caught the attention of the media. Mahatma Gandhi, who was preparing the nation for a civil disobedience movement against the British colonial rule, invited scientists and reporters from the industrialized nations to investigate the matter.

"A small group of scientists and reporters gathered in New Delhi and decided to travel with young Shanti Devi to Mathura. On reaching the town, they asked her to lead them to her husband's house. Through the narrow streets and alleyways, dodging pedestrians and cows, eight-year-old Shanti Devi led them to the house where she claimed she had lived.

"It was indeed the house where Lugdi and her husband had lived a happy married life in the past, and that is where she had died. She recognized the two sons who were much older but she but did not recognize the third son. He was also older than she was, and his birth had caused her death.

"Her husband asked her about the several gold rings he had given his wife Lugdi during their married life. Shanti Devi promptly responded that she had hidden them in a pot buried in the garden in the old home. To the surprise of the investigating team, they found the pot.

"Shanti Devi had asked where the large terracotta flower pot that adorned the entrance of the house had gone. The startled husband told her that it had broken. Shanti Devi went around the house and asked precise questions about the movement of furniture and her own living quarters.

"Later, little Shanti Devi was taken to her former mother's home. Lugdi's mother still lived there with her daughters, Shanti Devi's mother and sisters from her previous life. The old woman met with the young girl who claimed she was her dead daughter. The woman noticed the girl spoke like her dead daughter and knew things only she would know. Shanti Devi even pointed at some of the changes in the house that had taken place over the last ten years. At first, they did not believe her, but later, as Shanti Devi described her childhood with them in detail, they all broke down in tears and hugged each other. It was an extraordinary reunion.

"In the end, after a heart-rending farewell, the distraught child returned to her present home and began to readjust to her present-day family in New Delhi. Her heart, though, lay with her mother, husband, and sons of the previous life."

Tommy stopped reading from his notes as Spalding and Moira listened in rapt attention. They had not touched their food. They looked at each other in silence as they tried to grasp the full implication of Tommy's claim of a true story.

"Mary, mother of Jesus! What a tale!" Spalding was awed.

"What happened to Shanti Devi?" Moira, too, looked bewildered.

"Shanti Devi never married and retired as a government employee in New Delhi, India. She died in 1987 and even at that age, she found it hard to bury her desire to return to her family of her previous birth." Tommy replied, enjoying the attention of two grownups.

"You can go online, read about her, and even watch her interview," Tommy said proudly. "I can give you the URL."

"If past lives are a true phenomenon, it's a good thing we don't remember them." Spalding said thoughtfully.

"Unless…" Moira fumbled.

"Unless what?" Spalding asked.

"Unless something needs to be resolved." Tommy finished for her.

CHAPTER 16

The main headline read:

Exhume Sean's Body
Was It Murder Or Accident

The subhead was:

Tommy Says Sean Had Fractured
Index Finger When He Died.

Spalding and the editor stared at the headlines of the Daily Post that was about to hit the stands.

"This is a big gamble. We are going to make many people mad, especially the police department. But this could increase our circulation and the advertisers are happy."

Spalding smiled. He was inching toward his moment of glory.

"Poor Inspector Pasta. He was going to retire early next year, and now look at this," Spalding said with a smirk.

"I wish we could be sure," the editor mumbled.

"Uncertainty is the beauty of life. The only things we can be sure of are taxes, traffic, and thinning hair. That reminds me: I need a haircut."

"During office hours?" the editor snarled.

"Boss, they grows during office hours," Spalding said with aplomb before walking out.

⤋

The newspapers were buzzing with the story of Tommy as reincarnation of Sean, and so were the teachers and students. Whether they liked it or not, an obscure school like Thurgood Marshall Elementary was on the national radar, but it was for all the wrong reasons. Other newspapers had picked up the story, most of them ridiculing the whole notion of past lives and reincarnation. Some called it going back to the Dark Ages, when they burned witches at the stake. Others said the notion of reincarnation was similar to people thinking the earth was flat. Still others said it was as false as Columbus thinking he had found a western route to India.

The papers could not afford to ignore the story, but they had not sent their correspondents to investigate. This was partly because there was no evidence so far that Tommy was telling the truth or hallucinating and partly because Spalding had a tight lid on who talked to Tommy. Even Moira felt frustrated and humiliated when she read the headlines. Her so-called partner had kept her in the dark.

The new article caught Carol off guard. What she thought was a passing phenomenon had turned into a monster, and it was growing each day. Spalding had assured her that he would be the only reporter talking to Tommy. Spalding's egotistical, single-minded devotion to his byline ultimately proved a blessing to mother and son.

⤋

"What the hell do you mean, 'exhume the body'?" An infuriated Petrocelli waved the newspaper in Spalding's face. They were in the police office, where Spalding had gone to break the news gently. "What kind of journalism is this?

"Let's look at it this way. You have a chance to clear your name and retire peacefully. You did make a mistake by not ordering the autopsy on the Butler family," Spalding said calmly.

"And what makes you think I'm going to do it now, snoopy?" Petrocelli wanted to punch the insolent reporter.

"You'll do it. Otherwise the newspaper headlines will be screaming at the inept police department and your retirement will be tainted," Spalding said. "Tommy says Sean had a fracture in his right index finger before he was killed…"

"It was a drowning accident. What makes you so sure he's telling the truth?"

"A hunch. Besides, we all know you botched the investigation. Now you have a chance to absolve yourself. No fracture, no story, you win. I will publicly apologize, and your retirement will be smooth and free of drama. And I'll become the menacing paparazzi of tax-evading celebrities."

"I'll be damned if I—"

"You're damned either way, Inspector Pasta. Pick up the shovel and dig out the skeletons from your closet, or you'll become infamous for a botched investigation. Your career will be mentioned only in criminal justice textbooks." With that, Spalding walked out the door with Moira in tow.

The irate police officer held his head in both hands. He then picked up the newspaper and stared at the bold headline screaming for Sean's body to be exhumed. Petrocelli hit the desk with his fist as his assistant looked on.

"They didn't train us to deal with this past-life stuff. Why couldn't he wait six months?" The assistant nodded in sympathy.

❧

Spalding wanted to be the first to break the news to Tommy. He waited for him at the school gate. They both walked to the park across the street from the school.

"They're going to exhume Sean's body," said Spalding flatly.

"I want to be there."

"I don't know if it's a good idea."

"I want to be there."

"You're a brave boy."

"I have no choice."

Later that day at the newspaper office, Moira was visibly upset when she heard about the exhumation plans.

"I don't think there's any need for that. Besides, it's gross. I don't think his mother will allow that," Moira said.

"Life is gross. I married the same woman twice. Besides, Carol only has jurisdiction on her son, not on Sean Butler." Spalding put Moira's resistance to rest.

"When is the exhumation?"

"That's a secret."

"I'm very uncomfortable with the whole idea."

"Good. It's my job to toss people out of their comfort zone."

Spalding was on edge for days. He worried, thinking, *What if there is no evidence? What if the whole thing pops like a bubble? My peers would ridicule me. I will be a pariah.*

Tommy was anxious too. To take his mind off the impending event, he decided to restructure Leo's living space. He filled the dry aquarium with sand on one side and tiny pebbles on the other. He got a plastic container and painted it blue from the inside. He filled it with water and placed it in the middle. It was like a small oasis in the dry, rocky setting. He attached a ten-watt bulb to a battery. Turning off the bulb meant it was bedtime for Leo. The whole time he worked on recreating Leo's habitat, his mind was on the cemetery. He did not know why he wanted to be there, but he knew something needed to be resolved.

CHAPTER 17

It was early afternoon, and the sky was overcast; the wind was quiet, and the motionless trees stood like guards. The sound of shovels hitting the ground broke the silence in the cemetery. The cemetery caretaker exhumed Sean Butler's body with help from a few police assistants. Petrocelli stood nearby watching. Spalding was there, and standing behind him was a very nervous Tommy. Moira was absent.

Spalding was uneasy, and Petrocelli looked anxiously toward the cemetery gate. The tension was palpable. Spalding had gotten a court order to exhume the body. He had calculated that if there was any truth to the claims made by Tommy, then he was well on his way to the fifteen minutes of fame that was every reporter's dream.

Tommy nervously caressed Leo in his pocket. He was eleven years old and watching a body being exhumed. A body he claimed was his. Doubts and other scary thoughts assaulted him. What if they did not find that Sean had a hairline fracture in his right index finger? What if the whole thing was a yarn, woven from stray thoughts caused by diabetes and the tragic loss of his father? What if they put him in a psychiatric ward and declare him mentally ill? What if...?

No one noticed a black Volkswagen Beetle parked outside the cemetery.

It was a shallow grave, and soon the shovel hit the wooden casket. Two men tied a rope around the casket while the other two pulled it out of the grave carefully. Spalding and Tommy watched the decaying, muddy casket slowly surface and lifted above ground. As the casket was lowered, the man pulling the rope gave it a tug to let it rest on the ground, and the lid opened momentarily. A sudden gust of cold wind whipped the motionless trees, and the leaves rustled as if in protest. An inaudible cry passed through Tommy's dry throat. There it was: the decomposed body of Sean Butler. *Was it once mine?* He thought as he shut his eyes and stepped behind Spalding to avoid fainting.

The police officers carried the muddy casket to the van, to be taken to the forensic lab. The van that was usually rented to take the dead to the cemetery was now taking a deceased person back to society. Tommy's heartbeat began to normalize. Petrocelli wiped the sweat off his forehead, and Spalding breathed a sigh of relief. Everyone was glad that the gruesome task of unearthing a body was over. But they were in for another surprise.

As they were about to leave the dug-up site, a big dog with a dense white-and-brown coat came scampering to them. The dog stopped near them, and to their surprise, circled and licked Sean's gravestone. He then lay on its back, raised its legs in the air, and whimpered as if in mourning. Everyone watched the spectacle in disbelief. The dog's owner, a bald, middle-aged man with a double chin, walked slowly towards them. He wore blue, baggy pants and loose blue shirt, with grease marks on them. He looked vaguely familiar to Tommy.

"Hello, my name is Rupert Grossman. I'm an auto mechanic, and I work as a part-time janitor at the elementary school. This is Aussie," he said, pointing at the dog. "Aussie is an Australian shepherd. About twelve years ago, I got him from the kennel. I was told he belonged to Sean Butler, the boy who drowned with his family." As Grossman spoke, Aussie marched to Tommy and began to lick his shoes. He then looked up at Tommy and barked. Instinctively, Tommy knelt down and stroked Aussie's fur. The dog whimpered again, breathing heavily, the ageing dog buried his head in Tommy's legs.

Everyone watched the scene in stunned silence. The sight of a friendly dog calmed Tommy's nerves. Spalding's eyes shone with anticipation while Petrocelli sweated heavily.

"I've been reading about you in the papers. At first I didn't believe the story." Grossman paused. "Well, I still don't believe the story, but I can see he likes you. He's about thirteen years old and losing his vision. In human years, that would be about ninety-three." He waited for a response, but there was none. Everyone was speechless.

"You can keep him if you want. I was going to return him to the kennel or put him to sleep," Grossman said to Tommy.

Before Spalding could say anything, Tommy fondly caressed the dog, who again raised his head and whimpered.

"I'll keep him," Tommy said, rubbing Aussie's fur.

Am I lucky or a genius or both? A wave of excitement ran through Spalding as he imagined tomorrow's headlines. He shot a picture of Tommy petting Aussie beside the dug-up grave of Sean Butler, with the police and Grossman looking on.

⟣⟢

It was close to midnight. The town of San Felipe was in deep slumber. But some people were wide awake, all for different reasons. Petrocelli was pacing up and down in his office even though it was long past his normal work hours.

Spalding, wide-awake and giddy with anticipation, was drinking coffee and cognac. The TV was on, but his thoughts were elsewhere. *What if the whole thing blows up in my face? What will become of the irrepressible, congenital reporter I have become.*

"I hope I don't have to go to dental school or end up selling used cars." He frightened himself by saying aloud.

In his bedroom, Tommy was wide-awake and sitting near the window, staring at Aussie, who was dozing with his head between his paws. He was pleased that his mother had not made a fuss at having an addition to the family. She liked Aussie and felt the dog would be a good companion to Tommy. Nothing happened that night or the following day. An uneasy lull descended on all those involved with Tommy's story.

It was Friday evening, and Tommy was sprawled out on the sofa. He did not have any homework. He had not touched his tuna sandwich and salad. Tommy had fed Leo and placed him in his dry aquarium. Tommy washed his hands. The telephone rang, and Tommy dashed to the living room.

"So what's the result?" he asked.

"It's me." He heard his mother's miffed voice. "I was calling to see if you had eaten your sandwich, checked your blood sugar, and taken the insulin shot."

"Mom, I'm having the sandwich now." Tommy grabbed the sandwich and bit into it so he would not be lying to his mother. "And I will brush and floss my teeth. I have already checked my glucose level and taken the shot. Please don't worry about me," he implored.

Satisfied, Carol hung up, and Tommy half-heartedly proceeded to eat the sandwich.

"Leo, do you think they have the results at the forensic lab?" Tommy asked Leo. The lizard responded by wiping his large eyeballs with his long tongue.

CHAPTER 18

It was late at night, but the police forensics lab was well lit and very busy.

The lab was fitted with workstations that contained powerful microscopes and state-of-the-art DNA testing tools. A forensic specialist was at work on the exhumed body of Sean Butler. A technician was busy gathering tissue samples into a Petri dish. They had been working on Sean Butler's body nonstop for five days.

The examination process was in the last stages, as the specialist and technician examined tissue extracts from the body under the microscope.

"Hey, De Silva, come here and take a look," the specialist called to the technician.

The technician peered into the microscope and took a step back. They looked at each other meaningfully for a few minutes and then nodded. The forensic specialist made a quick phone call and proceeded to write the report.

Just then, the door opened and a pale, bleary-eyed, disheveled Petrocelli, entered the lab with his assistant in tow.

"Is the analysis complete?" Petrocelli asked.

"Yes, we were just finishing the report," the specialist replied.

"Well?"

The two scientists looked at him grimly. Their momentary silence spoke volumes. Inspector Petrocelli turned ashen.

"You found a fracture in the right index finger?" Petrocelli asked haltingly.

"No," the specialist replied.

Petrocelli heaved a sigh of relief, but it was short-lived.

"The hairline fracture is in the left index finger," the specialist said, looking at the data. "And that's the good news."

"And the bad news...?" Petrocelli asked hoarsely.

"There's no water in the lungs."

"Christ," Petrocelli said, barely audible.

"Death occurred due to possible strangulation, definitely not drowning."

"Hm, so now it changes from a possible case of botched investigation to a definite case of botched—" the assistant said.

"Silence yourself." The inspector snarled at his assistant. He then turned to the forensic team, and said, "I guess the FBI wants the other two bodies exhumed too."

The two scientists looked at him, and their gaze wandered to a corner of the room where two muddy caskets were already waiting to be examined.

"You're right." A tall man in an expensive suit walked briskly toward them. "Hello, I'm FBI Chief Greg Gomer. We take over from here. It clearly *was* a case of homicide that was not properly investigated because your department was in a hurry to proceed with a funeral instead."

A pregnant pause followed his introduction.

"Hope you are experts in déjà vu," Petrocelli said acerbically. The damage was done. He could breathe and engage in salvaging what was left of his reputation and retirement.

"We're experts. Period," the FBI chief said smugly.

⚜

Two weeks later, the newspaper announced that the forensic analysis had revealed that Mary and Philip Butler too had died of strangulation and not drowning. The small town of San Felipe was stunned. It had acquired notoriety for all the wrong reasons. The humbled inspector Petrocelli had conceded to shortcomings on his part and assured the FBI of his full cooperation in the rein-vestigation of the Butler family murder case.

"Mary, Mother of Jesus! Am I good or what!" Spalding, the real beneficiary of the surprise turn of events, was beside himself with joy. Tommy's story hit the national scene. The reporter had followed his instincts and unearthed a strange story of reincarnation that in its early stages had looked like a fairy tale.

He decided to celebrate newfound success with his colleagues and admirers instead of drinking himself to the hospital. The party at the newspaper office was raucous. He felt like a king as he held the newspaper with bold headlines.

Stunning New Revelation
Tommy's Past Life Claims Picture Perfect
What Next?

Tommy and Carol were the honored guests at the party. Surrounded by reporters and photographers Tommy felt like a celebrity. He felt some satisfac-tion in having his visions and dreams proven true. But he was uneasy about what the future held for him. Carol had mixed feelings as she smiled and talked to people. They both missed Frank.

Editor Goldstein was happy. He had gambled on his eccentric reporter and hit the jackpot.

"No photos or interviews without my permission." Spalding, like a swash-buckling hero, put his arms around Tommy and stood between photographers and the boy.

"I hold exclusive rights. All photos should be requested from our depart-ment and given proper bylines," he declared, much to the joy of his editor. The photographers and reporters from other newspapers looked sullen, but they could do nothing. They had tried to stake out Tommy's house, but Spalding had arranged a court order restricting their access. It gave the mother and son some reprieve from intrusive newspapermen.

"Hi, I'm Greg Gomer from the FBI," the chief along with his assistant, stood tall in front of Spalding.

Spalding was taken aback and glared at the editor.

"He invited himself." Goldstein shrugged his shoulders.

"We're glad you're working with the boy closely. We're seeking your coop-eration in solving this bizarre case." The uninvited FBI chief poured himself a beer and smiled at Spalding and the editor.

"But of course," the editor said. He knew instinctively that Spalding would be tough to move.

"I think you guys are old enough to earn your own livelihood." Spalding snarled at Gomer.

There was silence in the room as everyone realized that the Secret Service had found Spalding's Achilles heel. He jealously guarded his stories, sources, and byline.

"It's a felony to withhold information from a government agency," said the FBI chief with authority.

"Is that right? What about your shortcomings—all the unsolved murder, robbery and kidnapping cases? By the way, where did you bury the body of Jimmy Hoffa? And where were you vacationing when 9/11 struck."

"What?" The FBI chief turned red; his ears looked like fresh turnips. He was not used to defiance, but newspaper people were known to be wild boars.

"You have been living off the taxpayers, and now you want handouts from the media," Spalding was not done.

The chief turned to Tommy and Carol.

"Tommy, we'd like to talk to you. All information in the future should be directed to us." He gave Tommy and Carol a business card each. "Ma'am, we'll look forward to talking to you in the future. This case has taken a strange twist. Now it falls under our jurisdiction. We *do* expect cooperation from you and your son."

Carol was quiet at the sudden, somber exchange, and Tommy was about to say something, but Spalding winked at him.

"Que sera, sera, whatever will be, will be," Spalding sang in a loud voice. His colleagues were enjoying the drama.

The FBI chief, with his assistant in tow, turned around to leave when they bumped into Moira, who was entering the hall carrying files. She staggered and dropped some on the floor.

"Sorry, dear," the exasperated chief said as he exited in a huff.

CHAPTER 19

The morning drizzle turned into a nasty downpour, and the temperature took a dive. The school cafeteria was full of students. Tommy sat alone at his table. The skeptics and the critics were keeping their distance from him, and the school bullies, who disliked the attention Tommy was getting, looked angrily at him.

Outside the school premises, the news reporters and photographers lurked at a safe distance, waiting to take Tommy's photo.

Spalding had forbidden even Moira to talk to Tommy without his permission.

As Tommy swallowed his soup, he was distracted when the O'Flaherty sisters walked up to him with their food trays. They looked somber.

"The synonyms for *weird* are…" Sarah and Clara hummed like bees in unison, "*eerie, paranormal, menacing, ominous, scary, evil, peculiar, mysterious, uncanny, bizarre, alarming, strange, hair-raising, outlandish, wacky* and *off the wall.*" The twins then turned on their heels and walked back to their tables amid muffled laughter and guffaws.

Over at another table sat Tommy's former friends. Megan was not amused; Pete laughed nervously, but Johnny's response was the real surprise. "Shut up, Pete."

༺❀༻

At first, Carol thought it was creepy to have Aussie around the house. The dog that had belonged to Sean was maybe carrying memories of his old master. Sometimes she wished Aussie could talk like a human, if only for a minute. What stories he would tell; he was the only living being who knew all the secrets of Sean and his parents. Someone had found him scampering and barking on the spot where the incident happened and brought him to a kennel. Aussie was privy to what happened in those last moments. Dogs were capable of faithfulness, devotion and recognition. But Aussie also assuaged Tommy's loneliness.

"Honey, don't you need your friends?" she asked Tommy.

"Dad always said, 'Roll with the punches, gather strength, and when you feel strong, stand up and fight for what is rightfully yours.'"

"Love you, my dear." Carol, overcome by her son's sudden maturity, hugged him. "Your dad also said to keep the faith. There's a higher power that loves you and has given you life. Always remember that."

Bolstered by his mother's protective love for him, Tommy decided he was going to confront every adversary head-on.

He got the opportunity when the menacing O'Flaherty sisters approached him again in the cafeteria. It was lunch hour in the school, and students were crowding into the cafeteria. Tommy brought his tray to an empty table. Sarah and Clara approached him looking deadpan.

"Tell us about our past life, weirdo," asked Sarah, taking a seat opposite Tommy.

"Do you think we were twins in our past life, creepy?" asked Clara.

Tommy hesitated a moment and then decided to let them have it.

"In your past life, you were both nocturnal female raccoons who wrestled on my tin roof on full moon nights. You clawed and scratched each other for the neighbor's proud, macho male raccoon," Tommy said loudly, like he was telling a story.

"All that noise made me very angry. One night, I lit a fire in my fireplace, climbed the roof, held you both by your tails, and shoved you down the chimney. Then I ran inside and watched you roast alive in my fireplace. When you were well done, I pulled you out with a pair of tongs, chopped you into small pieces, sprinkled salt and pepper on you, and basted you with barbecue sauce. Then I fed you to the neighbor's male raccoon. After feasting on you, the male raccoon moaned and said 'insipid.'" Tommy was deadpan.

"Do you know the synonyms for *insipid?* They are *bland, flat, flavorless, unsavory, nasty, sleazy, anodyne, tasteless, seedy, disagreeable, distasteful, offensive, trite, disgusting, revolting, unpleasant, obnoxious,* and *repulsive.*" Tommy's voice resonated in a quiet cafeteria.

Sara and Clara looked stunned. A few tense moments passed, and the sisters suddenly burst into tears carrying their trays back to their table.

CHAPTER 20

The forensic examination of Philip and Mary Butler after their exhumation confirmed that their death was due to strangulation and not drowning. Spalding's position as a top-notch reporter was reinforced. Every shot in the dark turned out to be a bull's-eye. He got a raise and a promotion. Admiration and envy glowed in the eyes of his colleagues. At the same time, Spalding became more paranoid of byline thieves. He was reluctant to tell people his whereabouts. He would show up to work at odd hours and disappear when needed. He refused to cooperate with anyone who could beat him to the finish line.

"Here's your assignment. Make a list of all the events in the neighborhood immediately before and after the murders in 1995, especially the unsolved cases. I want all the details," Spalding told Moira as they walked through the busy financial district of San Francisco. They had been cooped up with the editor for an hour and were glad to be out in the sun.

"And what are you—"

"I'll do what I have to. I want strict secrecy and no mess-ups. We're going to crack the case before the FBI does. I want everything by Monday." His tone bordered on rudeness.

They reached a pedestrian crossing. The lights turned red.

"Today is Friday." Moira protested feebly, looking at the blue sky.

"I want it…"

Just then, Moira's cell phone rang, and a pretty woman walking into a bar distracted Spalding. He followed her. Inside, he noticed a man greeting her. Disappointed, Spalding walked back to the pedestrian crossing and joined Moira, who was still on her cell phone and had not noticed his ten-second escapade.

"Monday, for sure," said Spalding in a low voice. "And what are you doing over the weekend?"

"Your story, of course." A peeved Moira hailed a cab.

⚏

Monday evening was wet and chilly. Even the California sun was not immune to seasonal change. Moira arrived at Spalding's house in the early evening. She had been trying to contact him all day, but he had kept his phone off and stayed home. Finally when she was about to leave the office for the day, he asked her to come to his house.

When she arrived, she saw for the first time, the incorrigible reporter's den, the messy world of an eccentric. His living room looked like a valley where a herd of migratory bison had rampaged through. There were books and magazines all over. Yellowing newspapers were stacked up to the ceiling. Sticky notes covered the computer screen. Walls, doors, and even framed pictures had phone numbers written on them.

"You want to make some coffee?" he asked her. The kitchen was like a war zone, but she managed to make coffee.

"Okay, here is what I unearthed during the sunny weekend," she said, sipping her coffee. "I scanned the database of events that took place around that fateful day when tragedy struck the Butlers and spun the little town of San Felipe out of its touristy stupor." She looked at him for acknowledgement.

"Good advertising line. If you fail in this assignment you could always get a job with the travel bureau," Spalding sipped his coffee.

"Well, here is how it goes." Moira shuffled her papers. "On May 11, 1995, the day the Butler family disappeared…"

Spalding motioned for her to stop for a moment, walked to the stereo, put on his favorite Mozart, poured some cognac in the hot coffee, and swaggered back to the sofa.

"Life is good. Go on. So what happened on May 11, 1995?" he said nonchalantly.

Moira looked miffed. He always interrupted her when she was saying something important.

"There were three incidents around the town of San Felipe. There was an armed burglary in a liquor store on Eighteenth Street, at the corner of Washington and Jefferson. The second incident took place five miles down the road when a speeding car hit a mother of two. She suffered a broken shoulder and a concussion to the head. The third incident took place on Twenty-Fifth and Capistrano, where two men fought over a woman in a bar. Later, both found themselves in police custody with their wallets missing—"

"Stop," Spalding said unceremoniously. "On May 11, 1995, the great jewelry heist at the San Francisco Museum of Fine Arts happened about fifty-five miles south of here. Millions of dollars' worth of antique jewelry and rare coins were stolen and never recovered. Their estimated value at that time was thirty-five million dollars."

"The infamous jewelry heist?" Moira asked, looking surprised. "What has that got to do with the deaths of the Butler family?"

"Murders of the Butler family," he corrected her. "Petrocelli would not call it murder and look what happened to him." He closed his eyes for a moment and took in the music that filled the room. "It's been twelve years. The priceless jewels, now worth in excess of a hundred million dollars have never surfaced. Not even in the underground market," he said.

"These incidents seem totally unrelated—"

"Besides the jewelry heist, there were two separate car accidents near San Felipe that day. In one accident, three men in a black Mustang plunged to instant death in the Scottsridge Ravine. In the second, a gray van crashed half a mile up the road and burst into flames, killing the driver."

"Excuse me, how are the jewelry heist and the two separate car accidents related? Further, how could these three separate incidents be related to the Butlers?" Moira looked weary.

"The three men in the black Mustang and the man in the gray van that crashed each had a Scorpio tattoo on their upper right arm. They had been drinking like fish before they died within minutes of each other," Spalding said thoughtfully.

"Both cars were stolen, and the black Mustang was reported to be parked outside the museum, according to the police officer who wrote a traffic ticket."

"That's some research. How is it connected to the Butlers?"

"There was speculation that the robbery at the museum was committed by the Scorpio Gang." Spalding ignored Moira's compliment. "But there was no evidence, and no jewels were found on the four bodies or in their cars. Besides, all four died in bizarre automobile accidents within minutes of each other; it was very suspicious!" Spalding paused.

"They were rookie burglars who had no police records. They had pulled off a major heist without getting caught. That must have surprised them too. What do you think?"

"Nothing," she said flatly.

"What do you do when all four suspects are dead?"

"You play God. Take a handful of clay and water and create another suspect." Moira chuckled then immediately apologized. "Sorry, I didn't mean to make light of your investigation."

"Among the four dead men, Tanner and Karadzic were locksmiths," Spalding said, ignoring Moira's dig. "That explains how they were able to open a very secure locking device. Flynn was good with computer security systems, and the digital security system at the museum was compromised. Besides Drew, who was found dead, alone in the van, was a car mechanic. He must have stolen the two automobiles for the robbery."

"Wow."

"I'm absolutely sure the robbery at the museum, the Scorpio Gang, the Butler family murders, and these two bizarre auto accidents are connected," Spalding said, thinking aloud.

"What makes you sure?" Moira asked abruptly.

"Testosterone." Spalding glared at her angrily. "A sizeable amount in the blood gives men an edge when it comes to abstract thinking, logic, and manipulating spatial objects in the air. Textbook sexism, my dear; that's what makes me sure." He paced the room, looking uneasy.

"You're right, I should play God and create a fifth suspect," he added.

With that, he walked up to the stereo and increased the volume. The sound of Mozart's music filled the room, making it impossible to talk.

Tommy looked out the window at the morning sky. It was going to be cold. He put on his warm jacket and waited for his mother in the kitchen. They were going to have breakfast before she went to sleep and he to school. In the meantime, his eyes caught the headlines in the day's newspaper.

Forensic Analysis; Mary and Philip Butler Died of Strangulation

But Growing Speculation That The Robbery At The San Francisco Museum Of Fine Arts Twelve Years Ago And The Butler Family Murders Are Connected

As Carol walked into the kitchen, Tommy quickly folded the newspaper, gulped down his milk, and prepared to leave. She gave him a muffin and reached for the newspaper. Tommy took the muffin, tore out a part of the newspaper, wrapped the muffin, gave his mother a big hug, and walked out with his backpack. He did not want her to see the last headline.

Was Sean The Last Person To See The Jewels?

Tommy did not notice a black Volkswagen Beetle following him in the distance.

CHAPTER 21

P etrocelli had agreed to meet Spalding in his favorite bar.

"Let me buy you a beer," Spalding said as Petrocelli looked around at the nineteenth-century furniture and chandeliers.

"This bar withstood the San Francisco earthquake of 1906 while every building around it burned or collapsed to the ground," Spalding said.

The two adversaries had now come together to fight their common rival, the FBI. Once the forensics report had established that the Butler family was murdered, the FBI had moved into high gear. They had established the error Petrocelli's department had made, and now the police officer looked to Spalding for damage control.

"I believe the FBI wants to talk to Tommy," Petrocelli said.

"Yeah, but I'm not giving out freebies," said Spalding smugly.

"I guess you really want that Sunday TV show."

"Whatever." Spalding was surprised that the inspector knew of his ambition.

"Here are the papers." Petrocelli pulled out a sheaf of photocopies from a file folder and handed them to Spalding. Next, he unrolled a map on the table.

"This is where the van was parked before it skidded...I mean was pushed." He pointed to a spot on the map. "They were missing for seven days but no one noticed. They were camping here," he said before he took another sip of beer.

"It took us another two days to locate and pull out the van. Sean's body was discovered even later. We didn't see any sign of foul play..."

"Where was the van parked?" Spalding asked impatiently.

"Here, probably. When we pulled it out, it was facing north." Petrocelli put a finger on a specific point in the map.

"What's your assessment?"

"This is how we figured the scenario. The van was parked on an incline, and the Butlers were inside it while Sean played with the dog. The van slid into the lake because the brakes failed; the boy saw the van slip, he ran into the lake and tried to rescue his parents. He drowned, and his body was carried further downstream. Inside the van, the parents struggled but failed to escape, and they drowned."

"Any sign of a scuffle?"

"The door handles were on the floor of the car. We figured the Butlers tried to open the door, but the water pressure outside didn't allow them..." Looking embarrassed, Petrocelli paused and wiped the sweat from his brow.

"According to the forensics report, they died..." Spalding opened the file.

"Yeah, of strangulation. I know it like I know the national anthem. Look, it's a small town. We live and die simply. No one felt the need for an investigation."

"And the two auto accidents the same night not far from the Butlers?" Spalding reached for a different file.

"Yeah. I read your analysis." Petrocelli paused. "In my opinion, those were simply two bizarre auto accidents that happened within minutes of each other."

There was a pause.

"I was surprised you think the three incidents are related," the police officer concluded.

"Who's Joshua Gonzales?" Spalding pointed at a name in the file.

"He was the paramedic who pulled the bodies of the three drunken men from the black Mustang. According to him, two were already dead and the third died on the way to the hospital."

"The FBI never connected these two car accidents with the robbery?" asked Spalding.

"Nope. And those turkeys are paid twice as much as I am. Now they have to work from the déjà vu of an eleven-year-old. I love it. I'd like you to crack it before they do. That'll make my retirement sweet." Petrocelli sighed.

⸎

"So, what does Joshua Gonzales do now that he's retired?" asked Moira as she and Spalding drove out of town to the witness's house.

"He's a beekeeper," said Spalding as he turned on a dirt road leading to Joshua's house.

"I'm terrified of honeybees," Moira said, looking uncomfortable. "I hope he has them under lock and key."

The gate of Gonzales's house opened into a large, unkempt front yard. They could see the adobe house at the far end of the driveway. There were no other houses around. The nameplate 'Joshua Gonzales' at the wooden gate had honeybees buzzing over it. Underneath the nameplate was a big, dirty, wooden box. The sign on the box read Protective Gear Required. Spalding pulled out a protective suit and a beekeeping veil. He gave them to Moira.

"Are you sure we'll be okay?" Moira asked.

"I'm utterly unsure." Spalding was irritated. He did not know what to expect.

The two reporters walked nervously toward the house, where they could see the figure of a man covered in brown overalls. They got a little closer, and realized the man was not wearing any overalls; instead, he was completely covered with honeybees. There were several layers of bees buzzing over his body, including his face. His large eyes protruded through thick glasses.

"Hi, I'm Joshua Gonzales." He extended his bee-covered hand to Spalding, who cringed. The man smiled under the honeybees.

"This is a slatted rack. It goes between the bottom board and the brood chamber. This is where the queen bee can lay eggs and keep herself warm." Joshua Gonzales stood before a wooden beehive, holding a bee frame.

"I'm Derek Spalding from the *Morning Gazette*, and this is my assistant, Moira. I called and left a message..." Spalding politely ignored the queen bee as he introduced himself haltingly. In the last twenty years of reporting, he had come across many weird situations but never one this grotesque and dangerous.

"Yes, I know. So you're the reporter who's creating news." Gonzales enjoyed the unease of the reporters. "You know how the Spanish War started? A correspondent from the mainland, who had nothing to report from Puerto Rico, sent out sketches of imaginary atrocities the Spanish were supposedly doing to the native population. It changed public opinion and led to the Spanish–American War of 1898."

"I'm not that imaginative." Spalding tried to smile through the sticky screen of the beekeeping veil.

"You have two minutes before I let my bees out for a stroll. Please don't say or do anything that'll startle them, especially the queen bee. Mr. Spalding, you go first."

"About twelve years ago, on May 11, 1995, there was an accident on Scottsridge Ravine where a black Mustang fell into the gorge, killing all three men inside. You were the paramedic who pulled out the three bodies from that car. According to your report, two men were declared dead on the scene while one died on the way to the hospital."

"Yeah, I remember that accident. When I arrived at the scene, two men in the back seat were dead. I took one look at the driver and knew he wouldn't make it to the hospital, and he didn't. The front passenger seat was empty. The driver was conscious, but every bone in his body was smashed. Those guys had been drinking hard."

"Do you remember anything he said or did? Anything at all?" Moira asked.

"Nope. I put my mouth to his ear and said, 'Amigo, can you hear me?' The injured man whimpered. By the time we put him in the ambulance, he was stone cold. Here, take this." Gonzales gave Spalding a bottle full of honey.

"Take it for that boy, what's his name? Tommy Twiceborn?" Gonzales guffawed. Startled, the bees began to buzz furiously. Spalding and Moira got the message. Clutching the bottle of honey, they hastened to the gate.

Gonzales called after them. "You know, even today I think about it, and I'm not sure if the driver moaned or mumbled *Sam*."

Spalding and Moira dashed toward the car ahead of the furiously buzzing bees. Spalding pulled off the protective gear and threw it on the ground near the gate.

"Mary, mother of Jesus. A bottle honey and a whimper called Sam, maybe." Spalding said, throwing the bottle on the ground.

"A whimper indeed," Moira agreed with him. They rolled up the windows and drove out the gate.

CHAPTER 22

"C'mon, Aussie, let's go for a walk." Tommy pulled the dog's collar, but Aussie growled to show his discomfort and buried his head in his shaggy paws.

"Okay, if you don't want to join us, we will go by ourselves," Tommy warned Aussie, putting on his windbreaker and placing Leo in his warm pocket. As Tommy and Leo moved toward the door, Aussie slowly came out of his stupor and plodded up behind Tommy.

"Good. You need a nice walk on the sand and some salty air in your lungs," Tommy said happily, and together they left the house.

At the beach, Aussie's attitude changed. He ran around following Tommy's Frisbee and seemed to come alive with the smell of fresh sea air. Leo, too, loved the game but stayed securely ensconced in Tommy's pocket. The sea looked like an endless gray stretch; the beach was not crowded, but the setting energized Aussie.

"Hey, where are you going?" Tommy shouted as Aussie suddenly left the Frisbee and scampered out of sight.

"Aussie, don't play games. Come back," Tommy shouted again. But Aussie seemed to have disappeared behind the dark rocks that looked like wet granite.

"C'mon, Leo, go look for Aussie." Tommy took Leo out of his pocket and set him on the wet sand. "Go search for him and come right back to me," he commanded Leo, who gave one look at the foaming waves and the black rocks and chittered his disapproval. Tommy frowned. If there were a female gecko, Leo would go scampering after her. But today, with the wind whistling loud, he decided to stay with his master.

"Oh, fudge! You're no help, Leo," Tommy said, putting Leo back in his pocket and running in the direction Aussie had gone. "Aussie," he yelled again. And this time he could hear Aussie's bark in the distance.

"C'mon, Leo; I can hear him. Let's go look for him."

Leo stuck his head out like a guard, scouring the scene for Aussie.

"Aussie!" Tommy shouted, and this time the reply from Aussie was distinct but still distant. It came from a darkened cove where Tommy usually did not venture, at least not when he was alone. Tommy had no choice but to negotiate his way to the cove, hopping over foamy water, seaweed, and protruding sharp stones. He kept shouting for Aussie, and the slow growl of the dog guided Tommy into a gloomy cove where the smell of seaweed was pungent and visibility limited.

Tommy waited to let his eyes get accustomed to the dark. Then he saw Aussie scratching the wall of the cove. Tommy grabbed Aussie's collar and tried to drag him out, but Aussie growled angrily.

"C'mon, buddy!" Tommy tried to steer him out of the dark, but Aussie barked excitedly and snapped at Tommy's hand. He kept leaping at the wall of the cove.

"What is it, Aussie?" asked Tommy. Curiosity led him to peer closely at the cove wall. He brought out the penlight from his pocket. In its thin, sharp beam of light, he saw stones jutting out of the cove wall and strands of weeds in the crevices. At first, he saw nothing unusual, but as Aussie kept barking and pawing the wall, Tommy came closer and saw something odd: one stone stuck into the wall was different from the rest of the stones. It looked like an old, red, sandstone brick.

Instinctively, Tommy reached out to remove the brick. He pulled it toward himself, and after some effort, the brick loosened and fell. There was a dark hole, almost like a hiding place. With his heart beating against his chest, Tommy flashed his penlight inside the hole and was surprised to see a shiny object covered with moss and spider webs. Hesitantly, he reached inside and grabbed the object. Aussie's excitement was eerie. He barked and rolled on the ground, raising his four legs in the air, sending out a gut-wrenching moan the way he had in the cemetery. Tommy pulled out the round, metal object that was rusting and mossy. He rubbed the metal against the wall to remove the grime.

It was a thick, brass artifact in the shape of a snake biting its own tail. With a pounding heart, Tommy faintly remembered seeing that image in the chapter on Native Americans in the history book. It seemed someone had made the brass insignia into a belt buckle.

Tommy pocketed the brass insignia, dragged Aussie out, and walked toward home with a hundred questions running through his mind. *Who did it belong to? How did Aussie know about it? What is the significance of my finding the artifact?*

⁂

"We're blessed, my young friend," Spalding said, agog with amazement as he held the brass buckle in his hand.

"Are we?" Tommy asked, puzzled.

As Spalding stared at the shiny object, a million thoughts raced through his mind, among them images of hosting the Sunday news show. This was a momentous occasion. He felt exhilarated and complete as a reporter, ready to retire in a picturesque country house and write his memoirs. *I am on the right track*, he thought with satisfaction. How many reporters could say that?

"I would like to know who it belonged to." Spalding rubbed the brass object.

"Aussie led me to it," Tommy said, reflectively.

"Mary, mother of Jesus! Are you thinking what I'm thinking?"

"But we have no evidence."

CHAPTER 23

Moira typed the interview with the beekeeper on the computer in Spalding's messy house. She remembered the stickiness of the whole meeting and shuddered with discomfort. Spalding, with a drink in his hand, was glued to the movie *Malice* playing on television. His eyes sparkled at the part where Alec Baldwin angrily spouted the famous speech that started with "Yes, I'm God…"

"I have filed the interview with Gonzales, and it's dripping with honey," Moira said good-naturedly. There was no response from Spalding, and she decided to call it a day.

Next morning, it was a school holiday. Tommy accompanied Spalding to the newspaper office.

"Tommy, take my seat. Today is the day of initiation. I predict that one day you'll be a great reporter." Spalding turned to his coworkers. "Everyone here, give the young hero a round of applause and line up for autographs. This genie has doubled our circulation in a matter of months and turned me into the most dreaded reporter on the West Coast."

Everyone applauded loudly. Tommy liked being appreciated.

Just then, Moira walked in with that day's edition. Looking stunned, she read the headlines aloud.

Sam, The Fifth Man Is Key To The
Missing Jewels And The Butler Murders.

"Who's Sam? I thought we agreed it was the whimper of a dying man, not a real person," Moira said angrily. "Where's the evidence of a fifth person?"

"Remember when I complained that all four members of the Scorpio Gang were dead? You said create a fifth suspect. Now I have created Sam, the fifth man, out of thin air as per your orders."

"You're impossible." Moira was visibly upset. "How can you turn a dying man's whimper into a suspect?"

"I'm a white man, and what is white man's burden? To play God." Spalding responded loudly to a question with a question. The staff enjoyed listening to him.

"So you created a fifth person?" Moira asked, looking irritated.

"I am God, who has just created a creature called Sam, the elusive fifth man, from the whimper of a dying man. Just the way a woman was created from Adam's rib, on second thought." With that, he bowed regally to the applause and laughter of the entire staff, with the notable exception of his humiliated assistant and a reticent Tommy who was in a reflective mood.

Everyone in the newspaper office agreed that Spalding was in the wrong business. He should be exercising his public speaking skills in Hollywood.

"You have homework this week," Spalding said to Moira. They were walking toward a restaurant to have lunch. "You have to research the police records of all the Samson's and Samuels, anyone with the first name Sam. I have the password to the police database of criminal activity occurring in our multicounty area. This database includes the names collected over a fifteen-year period."

"That is classified information. How did you get access to it?"

"You're right, beautiful. But Petrocelli is under fire. He wants us to solve the case before the FBI further spoil his retirement," Spalding said smugly.

"I'm not going to follow up on a whimper."

"What!" Spalding snarled in the middle of the road. "Learn survival skills and do some real work."

"It's like looking for a needle in a haystack."

"Then use a metal detector."

Moira angrily stalked away. Spalding turned around and entered a bar.

"Women!" he looked up. "Now, if only Adam hadn't had a rib…but then who would make coffee for me?"

Moira called in sick for a whole week. She looked relaxed when she finally did show up.

"I'm sorry for my outburst. But then I was down with a virus and needed to stay home, rest, and take plenty of vitamins." Even though she apologized, Spalding could detect a strain of anger in her voice.

"I thought you wanted revenge for my creating the fifth man."

She ignored his remark. "Here is the information." "Okay, since none of the dead men of the Scorpio Gang had police records, I presume that our imaginary Sam also was a wannabe burglar, a novice of sorts. But to give you the benefit of the doubt, I have looked into the police records from before the great burglary took place. Three criminals with the name Sam had a police record before and after that fateful day in 1995. At the time of the crime, they were all out of prison. Now, twelve years later, one of them, Samuel Gish, is in a state run health facility and suffering from multiple sclerosis."

"So he' doesn't have a hundred million dollars in jewels."

"Exactly! The second, Samson Dana, has settled down in a trailer park in Modesto with his wife and three kids," Moira continued. "He works as a handyman in a lumber facility. He has difficulty making ends meet, gambles compulsively, and lives on state subsidies and food stamps. According to police records, neither of them have any tattoos. Maybe they removed them, or maybe the imaginary fifth man didn't have a tattoo," she said with a smirk but collected herself quickly and proceeded.

"He's not our Sam either."

"I agree. The third man is Sam Doughty. Now he's interesting. I was not able to contact him. He changed his name three times, mostly because he's a deadbeat father. And listen to this, his entire upper torso and his arms are covered with tattoos. Either he loves getting new tattoos, or he wants to hide that Scorpio tattoo. He has a pretty long criminal record. At present, he's MIA. No one knows where he is. He could be our man."

"Good work. Now how about that famous cup of coffee?"

"I think we could pursue Sam Doughty…"

"Maybe," Spalding said blankly.

Spalding had taken some pictures of Tommy and his pets at the beach where the boy had found the brass buckle. He now wanted some fresh pictures of Tommy against the backdrop of the school. Despite the curiosity and the excitement around Tommy, the school had decided to ignore the buzz. Carol and the school had obtained a court order to keep the media away from the premises.

"Tommy, I need a fresh photo of you holding the buckle. Just walk out the gate with the rest of the students, and I'll click," Spalding said, adjusting his camera.

"Hey, take our picture together." Megan walked quickly to Tommy's side.

"Okay, say cheese," Spalding said.

"Cheese is full of protein," Megan said sweetly putting her arms around Tommy.

"Good, I didn't know you had a friend." Spalding took a picture with his digital camera.

"I'll tell you when to talk to him." Johnny pulled on Megan's elbow.

"And who do you think you are?" said Megan angrily.

"I'm your big brother," said Johnny in his usual, bullying style.

"We're twins, remember."

"I came first," Johnny said authoritatively.

"No. Mom had a C-section. Besides, you nearly killed her when she was pregnant because you were weaker and taking her nutrients. Big brother, my foot."

"I'll kick your butt." Johnny was about to hit his sister when Tommy joined the fray and pulled him gently away from Megan. Johnny fiercely pushed Tommy away. He then pulled his sullen sister by the arm and walked in the opposite direction. Other boys nearby looked disapprovingly at Tommy.

The black Beetle slowly moved away from the school.

CHAPTER 24

It was late evening, and Tommy was feeding Leo fresh mealworms from a bowl. Aussie was on the floor looking sluggish. He was like a frail, old man who wanted to sit in an armchair and stare at nothing in particular. Aussie would become active when it was time to eat, but once his belly was full, he was back to his daylong siesta. That gave Leo all the time he needed with Tommy. Leo, though small, was a proud and territorial reptile. Every time Tommy tried to play with Aussie, Leo would run around the room, chittering in protest.

"Thank God Aussie is not a gecko, or you, my dear Leo, would have had a duel by now," Tommy said to Leo as the gecko flailed his long tail to show his appreciation for Tommy.

After eating, Leo slowly retired into the warmth of Tommy's shirt pocket to sleep until Tommy carefully carried him to the dry aquarium and placed him on the sandy bed. The television was on, and Tommy was drowsy. He had checked his glucose, taken a shot of insulin, brushed and flossed his teeth. He had finished talking to his mom and had gone through the checklist of all the chores he had to finish.

Tommy brought the smiling picture of his father, locked forever in the wooden frame, to the sofa.

"I miss you, Dad," Tommy said softly as he prepared to pull himself off the sofa and go to his bedroom.

Suddenly, the bland sounds of television turned into a happy cacophony of birthday greetings. The rendition of "Happy Birthday" filled the air. But that was not what startled Tommy. It seemed someone had turned up the volume, as the room reverberated with the sounds of cymbals, drums, and loud cheers.

Bewildered, Tommy watched the birthday celebration on the screen. A woman with her back to the camera arranged candles on the cake. She slowly turned around, holding the cake in her hands, and Tommy's heart beat fast. The woman was Carol. It was the first time he had seen the image of his mother on the screen. Tommy wanted to pinch himself to make sure it was not a dream or fantasy. But he couldn't move.

The kids onscreen sang happily to the birthday boy. Slowly, the birthday boy's face came into focus. Tommy let out an inaudible scream. It was him on the screen, dressed in a clean-cut tuxedo over a white shirt and a red bow tie, sprinting happily to the other kids. Suddenly everyone's expression changed to horror, and Carol's face twisted into a scream. Tommy on the screen followed their gaze to his left shoulder. There on his spotless shirt appeared a penny-sized red hole near his heart. The hole grew bigger and gradually soaked his white shirt in blood. Slowly, the Tommy on the screen collapsed in a pool of blood.

With a gasp, Tommy sprang from the sofa, his heart pounding hard against his chest and his mouth dry with fear. He reached for the remote. However, the television screen was already blank.

⧉

Next day, Tommy recounted the TV incident to Spalding, who listened quietly as they walked in the park.

"I don't know if I should have talked to you about this," said Tommy.

"I'm glad you trust me."

"Well, I can't talk to my mother, so that leaves you and maybe Moira—"

"The woman you saw on the screen, are you absolutely sure that was your mother, I mean, your present mother?" asked Spalding.

"Yes."

"She's Carol?"

"Yes."

"It's not an image from the past."

"No." Tommy was emphatic.

"If that is so, this would be the first time you have seen an image from the present and not from the past," Spalding said reflectively. "How many candles did you see on the cake?"

Tommy shut his eyes and recollected the scene. "There were two lit candles, the numbers one and two." Tommy opened his eyes. "It was my twelfth birthday."

"Then it's an image from the future," Spalding said casually and stopped. "Maybe you didn't get the numbers right. Maybe it wasn't a view of the future. Perhaps…" Spalding collected himself.

"Sean died before his twelfth birthday." Tommy trembled with foreboding as the meaning of that scene became clear to both. Spalding looked somber. Tommy turned around abruptly and ran toward home.

Spalding was in deep thought as he drove home. Tommy had asked him not to tell anyone about his latest vision. The boy did not want his mother to freak out, and the reporter was of two minds: should he hold the most important information from his readers who were now riveted to the story, or should he honor the wishes of the young boy who had come to trust him immensely? On the other hand, he was not sure if Tommy's experience was real. The boy was dealing with too much stress and his type one diabetes.

Spalding reached a decision as he arrived home. He had given his word, so he was going to honor it—at least for now.

CHAPTER 25

The sky was beginning to darken as Tommy rode home on his bike from the supermarket. The aroma of fresh bread in his basket wafted towards him. He had also bought Leo fresh mealworms from the pet store. Aussie dozed in the big basket that Tommy had attached to the back of the bike for him. Leo, as usual, perched himself in the warmth of his master's pocket. From time to time, he would peep out, enjoy the landscape, and then duck into the safety of Tommy's jacket.

For the past two days, the latest images from the TV still haunted Tommy. On the way home, he had to ride past the cemetery. He reached into his jacket, zipped Leo tightly into the pocket, and increased his speed to get past the dark area quickly.

Suddenly, as Tommy reached the gate of the cemetery, Aussie sprang out of the basket and scampered toward the cemetery. It all happened in a fraction of a second. One minute Aussie was dozing, and the next he was alert, as if given a cue to dash away to the cemetery. Before Tommy could do anything, the dog had disappeared.

"Aussie, come back," Tommy yelled. But there was no sign of the dog. Uneasy, he stood there not knowing what to do. Reluctantly, he parked his bike against the closed gate, reached to get his flashlight out of his backpack, and rolled under the weathered wooden fence to go inside. It was silent and eerie in the cemetery.

"Leo, go look for Aussie and send me a signal." Tommy unzipped his jacket and let Leo out while holding his flashlight. Leo walked cautiously inside.

"Aussie, come here! It's going to rain," Tommy called out again looking at the gathering dark clouds that partially covered the moon. Finally, he saw movement in the distance. He ran toward it and shone his flashlight. He spotted Aussie on his back with four paws in the air, sending out a familiar howl. Tommy moved forward and caught the leash.

"Leo, where are you? I am not here to play." Tommy flashed his light around, but Leo was not there.

"Darn, we don't even have an umbrella." Tommy groaned as he heard distant thunder.

The dog rolled on ground and then stood on his hind legs, looked up, and howled. Next instant, Tommy heard a slithering sound on the dry leaves and saw Leo climbing on top of a red headstone chittering loudly. Tommy shone the flashlight on Leo and stared at the stone. It was the headstone of Sean Butler.

Instinctively, Tommy reached out and lightly touched the inscription. A sudden gust of wind came from nowhere and picked up the dry leaves from the ground. He could swear he heard a moan. *Where did it come from? Was it a coyote or a dog, or maybe…?* He stared at the headstone with trepidation. His heart was in his throat. He felt a rustle near his legs and nearly jumped out of his skin. Then he realized they were dry leaves. His fingers felt wet even though it did not rain. Leo came chittering to him. He grabbed Leo ran and toward his parked bicycle on trembling legs with Aussie in tow. With a pounding heart, he rode to the safety of his home at breakneck speed.

Inside the house, he looked at the hand he had touched the headstone of Sean Butler with and let out a soft gasp. It had a trace of blood on it.

꧁꧂

The next few days were uneventful, but there was plenty going on in Tommy's head. He was sure that his life was taking him in some direction.

He had a mission. But no one could sit down with him and connect the dots between all the events in his life. He was estranged from his best friends. Leo and Aussie were not articulate. He wanted to keep his mother out of it. Spalding was obsessed with the next headline, the next scoop, and hosting a TV program in the future. The only person who would lend him an ear was Moira, but Spalding was so paranoid he had forbidden Tommy to talk to anyone without his permission.

Tommy missed his father. He brought his father's photo to the sofa. With moist eyes, he talked to the smiling image of his father. Frank's red hair and blue eyes sparkled through the glass.

"Dad, I wish you were here. There is so much going on, and I am unable to cope. Now I am more confused than before. I saw that strange birthday party on TV. Then I noticed fresh blood on my fingers when I touched Sean Butler's gravestone." He paused as if waiting for a response.

"What should I do, Dad?" Before Tommy could finish his sentence, the phone rang. It was his mom asking if he had done all the chores.

"Hey, Tommy, watch channel nine. They are debating UFO's. I think you'll enjoy the show," she said before hanging up.

Tommy turned on the TV and watched the show his mother suggested. One group of panelists was of the opinion that UFO's were real and that the government is deliberately keeping us in the dark. The other group said it was a figment of people's imaginations. The panel was made up of scientists, army personnel, astronomers, parapsychologists, and viewers who swore they had extraterrestrial experiences. Tommy watched in silence and suddenly perked up. He had an idea. Why hadn't he thought of it before?

"Thanks, Dad. That was quick." He kissed the framed photo of his father. "And thanks, Mom." Tommy blew a kiss to his absent mother.

CHAPTER 26

It was morning, and Aussie was asleep in his big basket. But Leo jumped into Tommy's bed, swishing his tail. Usually that meant, "Let's go out and have fun." Tommy set the gecko on the desk and talked to him.

"Leo, today I'm going to meet someone interesting, and I can't take you with me."

But Leo kept chittering and would not let up. Then Tommy noticed something odd with Leo's long tail. The shell of the old tail was coming off. The gecko was wriggling to shed the bulky thing while a new tail emerged from under the old one. Excitedly, Tommy peeled the old skin off, looked at the gleaming new tail, and smiled.

"Congratulations, my friend. You look handsome." Leo swished his new tail happily and chittered at the compliment. Tommy placed the disappointed gecko back in his dry aquarium.

"I know you want a partner. We'll just have to find you one in California instead of in the Himalayas," Tommy said sadly. "I've told the pet store owner to look out for a suitable female leopard gecko. Now cheer up," he said as he stroked Leo's new tail.

After school, instead of heading home, Tommy cycled toward the hub of the town and followed the directions he had found earlier. Finally, he located the tall building he was looking for. He took the elevator to the second floor and stood before the glass door with the sign, Massey Institute of Parapsychology.

"Good afternoon, ma'am. I'm Thomas Stevenson," Tommy said to the receptionist.

"Thomas, you may go in. Professor Kipling is waiting for you," said the receptionist, looking a little surprised. She had expected someone older.

Inside, the professor's room was like a small warehouse of old and new books. The bookshelves were spilling over with books, files, and folders. There were books stacked in the corner of the room reaching up the ceiling.

Professor Kipling himself looked like an old book ready to dispense knowledge. He was a wiry man, with very salt and pepper hair and dark beard and moustache. The old man stared warmly through his large, black-rimmed glasses at the young boy who cautiously took a chair opposite him.

"I've read everything about you, Thomas Stevenson. You're very interesting. Now, what can I do for you?"

"I believe you have done research on reincarnation. I want to know what it means to you. Why some people remember their past lives while others don't?" Tommy read from the flash cards he had prepared.

"Many people have past-life experiences. Presently there are two hundred to three hundred validated cases worldwide, where people have accurately recalled their previous lives." The professor took out an unlit pipe from the drawer and held it between his teeth.

"A large number of these are children." He smiled his warm, affectionate smile. "I was not in the least surprised when I heard that you were eleven years old and remembered past life events. In fact, according to research, children as young as two years old begin to recollect memories of another life." The professor inhaled from an unlit pipe.

"Why do some remember and others don't?"

"In my research, I have discovered that the most prominent recollections of a previous life has to do with the moment and manner of death. In most cases, the death was abrupt or violent. That moment lingers in the transmigration of memory to the next life. The intensity of past experience strengthens the present fixation or memory, which is then triggered by sensations or images in this life."

"Is there something common in their stories?"

"Yes. According to documented cases, visions from a previous birth commonly occur among those whose lives ended in childhood or youth. They are more likely to transport the traumatic memory into the next life. They carry sharp and sometimes accurate images of a past life into a new birth. The moment of death, which in most cases had been sudden, is prominent in these cases."

"Is there a reason why they remember those events?" Tommy was excited.

"According to the Hindu and Buddhist beliefs, reincarnation is an opportunity to learn and grow spiritually. They believe it happens because of some unresolved business that needs closure. It could be deep attachment to a loved one, an unfulfilled desire, or an incomplete task." The professor adjusted his square glasses, taking a long drag from his pipe, which was still unlit.

"Do events repeat themselves in the person's next life?"

"They may follow the same pattern, but as to the exact replication, we don't have enough data. Why?" Professor Kipling peered at him.

"I think I'm going to be killed again before I turn twelve, just like last time. I saw it on TV," Tommy blurted out, and his intensity startled the professor. They stared at each other. A gust of cold wind blew some papers off the table. The professor began to collect them from the floor. Tommy, numbed by his own outburst, exited the room.

A black Volkswagen Beetle followed him at a distance.

CHAPTER 27

During the next week, Tommy had two new visitors.
It was a brisk autumn day; some trees stood naked, while others were a riot of colors. If Tommy could have calmed his mind, he would have appreciated the beauty of nature.

The school bell rang, and Tommy walked to the gate. He was delighted to see his mom. Sometimes his mother surprised him by arriving at school unannounced. It meant they would go see a movie or have a special treat. Then he saw something he did not like. His mom was in conversation with Rupert Grossman.

Tommy was grateful to Grossman for giving him Aussie, and he loved Sean's dog. But something told him Grossman was not there by chance. He waited for the man to leave, and then raced to his mother.

"Hi, Mom. What a surprise! What was that man saying to you?"

"Oh, nothing. He wanted to know if he could borrow a climbing gear," Carol said, walking to the car. "He was generous enough to give you the dog. Is it okay with you if I lend him the gear?"

"Of course, Mom'," Tommy said with relief. He did not tell his mother that if he had not taken Aussie from Grossman, the dog would have been put to sleep by now.

Tommy knew Grossman was not there because of the climbing gear. He followed his intuition and began organizing the data on his computer. Tommy changed the names of the files, the usernames, and the passwords to protect his private and mysterious world more securely.

Two weeks passed, and Tommy did not think much of his mother's meeting with Grossman until one day he came home and found the man snooping around their living room.

"Hi, Mr. Grossman, can I help you?" Tommy asked.

"Hello, young man. How's Aussie?"

"Aussie's great company. Can I help you?"

Carol called from the kitchen, "Honey, I was waiting for you. Take him to the garage. The stuff he wants is in the green duffle bag."

"This way, sir," Tommy said as he pointed to the garage.

"Young man, my computer's down. May I check my e-mail first?" Grossman asked.

Reluctantly, Tommy led Grossman to his room upstairs. The man was invading his private world. He turned on the computer and waited for it to boot up.

"Thanks, Son, I won't be long," Grossman said, hinting that he did not need Tommy in the room. That was enough to raise Tommy's suspicions.

Tommy left the room and shut the door behind him. Once in the hallway, Tommy opened his homemade periscope and extended it. Through the glass pane above the door, he could see the janitor, and what he saw confirmed that his suspicions were valid.

Grossman quickly inserted a flash drive into the computer and started to download files randomly. As the files were downloading, Grossman searched in the drawers, behind the books, and under the computer. He noticed a sticky note that said "password" and quickly slipped it in his pocket. Ten minutes later, Grossman was down in the living room.

"Did you check your e-mail?" Tommy asked.

"Yes, thank you."

"The climbing gear's in the garage."

"I'll take it next time." Grossman whizzed out the door.

Tommy smiled. Grossman was unaware that Tommy had turned the Internet off.

"C'mon, Aussie, let's have some fun." Tommy dragged the sleepy dog into the basket behind the bicycle and sped to Grossman's house. When he reached the unkempt house shrouded in foliage, he hid behind the thick bushes and slowly inched forward and peered through the kitchen window. Grossman had inserted the flash drive into his own computer. He scanned the files and opened a file named Tommy's Secrets.

A Password Required prompt appeared on the screen. Pleased with himself, the janitor pulled out the sticky note from his pocket and typed in the password. A message appeared: Wait, Your Password Is Being Verified. Slowly, a picture of the backside of a gorilla began to download on the screen with the words "Gross Man." The janitor looked stupefied. Realizing he had been fooled, he cursed loudly and kicked the desk. Tommy, hiding outside, chuckled, grabbed his bike, and rode away from the angry man's house as fast as he could. He was sure Grossman would not approach his mother again.

⁂

A few days later, a second visitor surprised him. A young man stepped out of a black Volkswagen Beetle and rang the bell at Tommy's house. Once inside, he introduced himself as Chad and began to yell at Tommy.

"You've no right to disturb the dead with heathen ideas," Chad said angrily to Tommy. He was dark and handsome, and in his early twenties. He had an athlete's body but was dressed in a black jacket and pants, and wore a priest's white collar. He had an uneasy intensity in his eyes and looked troubled. Tommy was struck by the deep worry lines on the young man's forehead.

It surprised Tommy when Chad rang the bell and walked in nonchalantly as if he were an old friend of Tommy. In a way, he was.

"Sean was a timid student," Chad told Tommy. "In school, we shared a desk, and he would let me copy his homework. I was rough on him sometimes, but he never said a word. Once he didn't let me copy his homework. That made me angry, and I poked his arm with a lit cigarette I had stolen from my dad."

"Ouch, that must have hurt."

"Sean never said a word. I was going to apologize, but it was the last day of school. I thought I'd wait until the next semester, but he was gone." Chad pulled Tommy's sleeve up and peered at his arm.

"Right here. If you don't remember, you can't be Sean Butler."

"What else do you know about Sean?"

"You're just trying to be this big shit, getting your picture in the newspaper." Chad ignored his question. "Besides, the ideas you're spreading are heathen, according to the Bible." He produced a Bible from his pocket. Tommy stared at the book.

"I'm training to be a priest," Chad said.

"If you weren't training to be a priest, what would you want be?"

"A football player. That's what I'm good at." Chad's eyes sparkled. "That's what my girlfriend—I mean my ex-girlfriend—wanted me to pursue, but all that is in the past now. I just came to tell you that you should stop telling lies and spreading these non-Christian ideas…for your own good," Chad said seriously. He turned around and stepped out the door just before Carol entered.

"Who was he?" Carol asked, looking exhausted.

"A classmate."

"So tall," Carol said, wearily walking into her bedroom.

"Poor Mom." Tommy sighed.

⟨�⟩

Chad slept in his unmade bed in a messy studio apartment. The walls were bare except for the wooden cross that hung prominently on the wall above the mantle.

On his bedside table, there was an empty bottle of alcohol, a Bible, some white powder, and the crumpled picture of a young woman on the floor. Chad tossed and turned in the bed, mumbling incoherently, then woke up with a start.

Stepping out of the bed, he turned on the lights and rummaged through old books, papers, and files in his desk drawers and pulled out a handbook titled *George Washington Elementary School Art Projects 1995*. He flipped through the pages and stopped on the page where sixth-grade students had displayed their artwork. A picture of Sean Butler holding a round brass insignia in the shape of a snake biting its own tail was at the bottom of the page. The caption read 'Aztec Ouroboros', a Native American artifact symbolizing eternity, continuity and rebirth." It was the same insignia he had seen on Tommy's belt.

Tears welled up in his eyes as he stared at the picture.

CHAPTER 28

It was morning, and Tommy had to go to school. He stepped out of the shower and dried himself in front of the mirror. He noticed something odd. He put on his pants and climbed down the stairs, carrying his shirt.

"Mom, what's this," Tommy raised his arm and showed Carol the penny-sized bruise that he had just discovered.

"Oh honey, that's a birth mark. It was reddish and noticeable when you were a baby. Now it seems to have grown with you and blended in with your skin," she said, putting dishes in the dishwasher. "Why do you ask?"

"I just noticed; that's all." Tommy put his T-shirt on.

He had so much to tell Spalding and Moira.

It was late afternoon, and the sun was casting an orange hue on the sky. The wind slowly picked up speed, and the rustle of dry leaves turned into nature's melody. The sounds of loud laughter came from inside Spalding's house. Both Spalding and Tommy cackled. Tommy had just narrated the Grossman episode, and Spalding could not contain himself. When Moira entered, Spalding was on the couch indulging in a deep belly laugh.

"Grossman turned into a shaggy dog story. Tommy, you're smart, and I love you."

"Hey, what's the joke?" Moira asked, looking puzzled.

"Who's laughing? We're very serious," Spalding said, pursing his lips.

"Tell her, Spalding. It's about Grossman." Tommy did not like to make fun of Moira.

"You tell her. I'm busy enjoying myself." Spalding guffawed.

"Well, you see, Grossman tried to make friends with my mother. He came to my house on some pretext to download files from my computer." Tommy chuckled.

"And you both find that funny? That's alarming." Moira was annoyed, but Spalding let out another chortle and laughed till he had tears in his eyes.

Late evening after everyone was gone, Spalding puttered around the house in a reflective mood. He turned on his favorite music, set some coffee to brew, and tried to tidy the living room table but decided it was an impossible task. He watered the plants and settled down on the sofa with a coffee mug.

He then groped under the cushion of the sofa, pulled out an old brochure, and stared at it for several minutes. It was a brochure from the San Francisco Museum of Art in 1995 with pictures of antique jewels. Gently he ran his hand over the dazzling pictures and smiled.

"Speak up, beauties. Where are you?" Reclining on the sofa, Spalding began to think seriously. There was a battle going on in his mind. He began to write on a piece of paper. It did not make sense. He paced up and down the living room with a cigarette, sending out smoke rings into the air; that did not help either.

"Should I, or shouldn't I. That is the question?" He mumbled. The conflict between ethics and ambition was fierce but short. In the end, ambition won; he was going to keep his interest above everything else. He stared at the poster of the Sunday TV news show.

"Mary, mother of Jesus, I won't be the first reporter who's ruthlessly ambitious," he said loudly, settling down on the computer to write his article.

CHAPTER 29

A stounded, Tommy read the newspaper headline.

Tommy Knows Where The Jewels Are

He read the entire piece in shocked silence.

"He shouldn't have done this," Tommy mumbled to Aussie, who stood by and growled. Leo was standing right on top of Aussie, flailing his new tail. Just then, the telephone rang. Tommy darted for it before Carol.

"Hey, young man, how are you?" Spalding said cheerfully.

"I don't feel good about that article. I don't have a clue where the jewels are. I don't even know if there were any," Tommy said, all in one breath. "Mom would be mad if she read the newspaper."

"Don't worry, young man. Trust me. I will not let any harm come to you."

Back at the newspaper office, Moira picked up the newspaper and read the headline. She slapped the paper on the desk and found herself staring into Spalding's face.

"A shot in the dark, as usual?" she exclaimed.

"You bet," Spalding said nonchalantly.

"So where's the booty?"

Spalding pulled both his empty pockets out of the pants and let them hang loose. "Patience, Sister. Patience. You'll be the first one to know where the glittering gold is. I promise. Till then, mum's the word."

"I have been working on this case day and night, and you didn't take me into confidence. I thought we were partners." Moira was hurt.

"Partners my foot. I'm your big brother, but first, that famous cup of coffee, sister," he barked.

"Even if it's true, which I doubt, you haven't done that little boy a favor," Moira said as she rose from her chair.

Tommy did not have a good feeling about Spalding's new announcement in the newspaper. He had no clue where the jewels were. Even the idea of a hundred million dollars' worth of jewels was foreign to him. He was not sure if Spalding was doing the right thing by connecting the antique jewelry heist to the murder of the Butler family. Both events happening on the same day was nothing but coincidence. They happened within a fifty-mile radius of each other, but that was not enough to connect the two.

These and other thoughts churned in Tommy's mind as he walked slowly toward home. He had stayed at school longer than usual to finish his art project and was returning home without the regular hustle-bustle of other students going home. The road was deserted. The sky was overcast, and the evening was threatening to turn dark soon. He thought of his mom, who would be up soon, and increased his pace.

Just then, he felt someone behind him. He looked back, but the street was deserted. There was no one, but his sixth sense warned him to get home as soon as possible. As he increased his speed, he again felt someone behind him, not close, but definitely following him. This time he saw a shadow disappear behind a side lane as he looked over his shoulder. Any kind of stress led to a sudden spike in his sugar levels, and Tommy felt his mouth turning into sandpaper. From the corner of his eye, he saw a shadow leap behind a large house.

With his pulse racing, Tommy decided to hide behind a bunch of bushes that grew wild around the road. He crouched behind the tall shrubs and tried to see who the stalker was. Holding his breath, he waited in the bushes for a few minutes. He saw no one. Maybe he was just being paranoid. He waited a few more minutes and decided to come out of the bushes and head home.

"Shh." Someone pulled him back with a whisper.

Sweat appeared on Tommy's forehead. He turned around and was relieved to see Moira.

"Thank God it's you," he whispered. "I thought I was being followed."

"Quiet. You are," she whispered back. "Wait here, and don't come out until I tell you." She stepped out of the bushes, walked up the road, and looked down the side road. It was deserted. She lingered for a few moments and came back to Tommy.

"Come out. Whoever he was has gone. Why are you going home so late?"

"I had to stay back and finish my art project. What are you doing here?" Tommy asked, breathing a sigh of relief.

"Well…" She hesitated. "Actually, I thought I could catch Grossman and have a word with him. May I drop you home?"

"Thank you, Moira. Thank you for saving me," Tommy said, and before Moira could say anything, he ran home as fast as his could.

⁂

"Why the hell did you have to go sneaking up on Grossman?" Spalding yelled after screeching to a halt in his driveway.

"I thought it would be prudent to have Grossman under observation," Moira said feebly.

"Who asked you to *think*? Besides, what if Grossman comes after you for stalking him?" Spalding was so mad he stood in his driveway and slammed her with questions.

"I was shocked that he tried to steal Tommy's files and password. And all you did was laugh," Moira said softly.

"Yeah, and look how an eleven-year-old was able to fool the congenital janitor."

"I'm sorry. I should have asked you." Moira felt deflated.

"I've already checked him out." Spalding softened a little at her apology. "He's a petty con artist who has not been successful at anything. Now let's have some coffee." Spalding searched for his keys in his pockets.

"Mary, mother of Jesus. I'm locked out again." Frustrated, he hit his fist against the door. "Why do I keep forgetting things I'm not a professor?"

Spalding led Moira to the back of the house where the grass was as tall as the master of the house. The bougainvillea tree covered the back wall of the house completely. Under the shadow of the wild growth, there was a hummingbird feeder. Moira felt it was odd that it was behind the dense tree, making it inaccessible to birds. Spalding reached for the feeder and tugged the chain gently to the left, and then to the right.

Moira was surprised to see the feeder was secretly attached to the window of his first-floor bedroom. Spalding winked at Moira and slowly pulled the feeder toward himself. There was a sound of a latch opening inside, and Spalding pushed the window open and climbed into his bedroom.

"Honey, I'm home," he announced as he entered his bedroom. "Oh, that's right. My ex-wife lives in Boise, Idaho." He put on his favorite classical music and poured himself a drink. Holding a drink in his hand, he sauntered back to the window where Moira was still waiting for him. Amused, Spalding grabbed her arm from across the window.

"What's the last wish of a dying man, who, all his life was obsessed with calories?" he asked with a mischievous grin.

Moira looked puzzled, her hand still in his.

"Diet soda." He laughed loudly as she still looked puzzled. "I could open the front door for you."

Moira turned red up to her earlobes. She then went around the house to the front door and walked in, looking embarrassed.

"I'll check my e-mail while you make coffee."

"Sure." She puttered in the kitchen then returned with two coffee cups. He minimized the screen as she approached him.

"I wasn't looking at your e-mail," she said, looking hurt.

"Come, let's talk." Spalding ignored her remark. "Do you have a boyfriend?"

"Not in a long time."

"How is that possible? The only other person I know who does not have a steady partner is me." Spalding looked into her gray-blue eyes. "Even though you have not done anything spectacular to compete with me, I would say you *are* full of possibilities."

"Hm."

"You could be included in a story titled *Women Who Made History*." He looked intently at her. "Like Godiva of France, Helen of Troy, Bloody Mary of Scotland, and Phyllis McMahan of Boise, Idaho."

"Phyllis McMahan?"

"God created these women from man's rib to tickle him from time to time. Instead of doing their job of amusing men, they caused major spinal injury to history itself," Spalding said, ignoring her quizzical look.

"Who's Phyllis McMahan?"

"My first and second wife." Spalding handed her the cup. "You make excellent coffee."

"I think you're an ambitious man, a natural reporter, but a true misogynist who is terrified of women. I feel sorry for you." Flustered, she picked up her jacket and left his house.

CHAPTER 30

Tommy paid a visit to the drugstore and bought a dozen small pieces of cosmetic mirrors about two inches by two inches. He then taped three mirrors along the wall in each corner of the room. The mirrors were taped in such a way that image in one mirror was reflected in the adjacent mirrors. This allowed him to look at everything from any angle without moving or turning around.

He had been uneasy since the false piece of news Spalding put in the newspaper claiming Tommy knew the whereabouts of the jewels. It was bad enough to be connected to the murders and robbery. However, to be privy to the whereabouts of millions of dollars of antique jewelry was too much for him, besides it was a lie.

It was a cold evening with intermittent showers. Tommy was in his room working on his homework assignment. The doors and windows were closed. Aussie was dozing on the carpet with his head between his paws, and Leo the glutton was nibbling on bits of chips and cheese. Carol was downstairs, cooking and watching TV. It was her day off. There had been a lull in the sequence of events related to Tommy. For Carol, every pause brought respite, and she wished for more.

Suddenly, Tommy was alarmed as he noticed a shadow in the little mirrors he had fixed onto his walls. He became aware of something or someone other than Aussie, Leo, his mom, and him in the house. The TV was on, and he could hear his mother cooking in the kitchen. It was unlikely she was near his room. Slowly, Tommy looked up in the mirror in front of him and saw the shadow again.

"Aussie," Tommy called out softly, but Aussie buried his head in his paws with a reluctant moan. Leo came scampering to his master, but the gecko could not do much. Tommy, his heart beating hard against his chest, held Aussie by the collar and dragged him to the window.

"Who's there?" he said softly and then repeated loudly. "I said, who's there?"

There was no response. Suddenly he heard a rustle in the bushes outside. Sensing there might be someone on the patio while his mother was alone, Tommy dragged Aussie downstairs and ran across the living room, opened the patio door, and yelled.

"I know you're there."

The silence was deafening. But just as Tommy thought he was being overly suspicious, there was a crashing sound and shuffling feet. Tommy looked in the direction of the sound and before he could make any sense of it, something or someone jumped at him, throwing him off balance. He felt fur, nails, and a loud snarl. Tommy screamed, Aussie barked, and Leo chittered loudly. Tommy looked at what had hit him. It was his neighbor's big, lazy tomcat growling in displeasure. It took a moment for Tommy to realize what had happened. That cat had never bothered Tommy before. He was a friendly feline, but it seemed someone had grabbed the cat and thrown him at Tommy, perhaps to distract him.

"Who's there? Who the hell's there?" Carol, with a bottle in her hand, came out yelling. "It's my night off. If you're sick, go to the hospital. If you're dead, go to the mortuary." She then turned around to her son, who was shaking with fear.

"You okay, honey?"

"Mom, he was here. Sam was here. He wants to kill me. I swear I don't know where the jewels are, Mom. Spalding put that in the newspaper just to rattle someone out there. And now Sam, the fifth man is after me, and he'll kill me again." With tears running down his cheeks, Tommy hugged his mother tightly.

"Help me, Mom."

People do things and rarely anticipate the consequences of their actions. Spalding was no exception, for he had only thought about how his actions would land him on the prestigious TV show he had been dreaming of hosting. Creating a fifth man out of thin air was a calculated risk, based on an unreported piece of evidence, a whimper Gonzales thought he heard twelve years ago.

The story that Tommy remembered the whereabouts of the jewels was a blatant lie. It was unethical, and Spalding had not taken anyone into confidence, including Moira and the editor.

Late as usual, Spalding entered the newspaper hall and immediately sensed tension. He rubbed his stubble, heaved his briefcase on his desk, looked around at the tense faces, and walked to the editor's room.

"All right, let's get over with it," he said and slammed the door behind himself.

Inside, he was surprised to find Inspector Petrocelli, Carol, and a very grim editor. Before Spalding could decipher the situation, it was out of control.

"You son of a bitch. You risked my son's life for a fabricated story." Carol lunged forward and slapped him on his face. "You used Tommy as live bait." She spat in his face.

"Mrs. Stevenson wants to press charges against you for endangering her son's life based on a false report," the editor said gravely. "Tommy would submit in writing that he never said anything about the missing jewels."

"Charges? I want to shoot the scumbag!" Carol tried to pull the gun out of Petrocelli's holster.

"Please, Mrs. Stevenson, that's my job." The inspector restrained her.

"If I see you around my son again, I'll kill you with my bare hands. I don't need a gun," Carol yelled at Spalding and pushed past him to the door with the inspector in tow.

Silence filled the room after the unceremonious departure of Carol and the inspector. No one had expected things to get out of control with such intensity. Spalding was shaken, but he maintained his cool.

"I know you're hustling for the story, but I will not have the newspaper shafted for false statements. You will apologize to her in writing or drop this assignment completely," Goldstein said grimly.

"I was right about Sam," Spalding said with a twinkle in his eye.

"You will *not* endanger the life of the boy. Do you understand?" the editor said loudly.

"I smoked him out. The fifth man exists," Spalding said triumphantly. "Am I a genius or what?"

"I'll persuade her not to press charges. Apology, in writing. Is that clear?" the editor thundered.

"Sam is in town. It worked. Don't you see? I laid the trap, and he took the bait." Spalding turned to exit when the editor spoke again.

"I repeat: I want you to write that note of apology. One more thing: what's between you and Moira?"

Spalding stopped abruptly and mockingly raised his right hand to his heart. "Coffee. Nothing but well-roasted Colombian coffee shipped directly by the cartel. So help me God."

"She says you've reduced her to a gofer, you don't appreciate her work, you're secretive, and you make her insecure." The editor slapped Moira's complaints on Spalding.

"I appreciate her coffee. That's security," Spalding replied in his typical inimitable style.

"Don't be a chauvinist; she was keen to work with you at first."

"What? I thought you put her to spy on me."

"She was hired the day you broke Tommy's story. She expressly wanted to work with you. I guess you earned yourself notoriety after you solved the Kirby murder case. She's your admirer, not your competitor."

"I'll be damned. Why didn't you tell me earlier?"

"You're overly suspicious, which makes you chicken."

"A daily dose of suspicion and alcohol keeps a man alert," Spalding said and reached for the door, but then he turned around, frowning.

"My gut tells me to be wary of her."

"Don't forget to apologize to the boy's mother in writing. Now get out and let me get on with my business."

❧❦❧

The sky was overcast, and there was a slight nip in the air. It was lunchtime, and the financial district of San Francisco was teeming with people.

Moira wearing a long black coat, a black hat, and black glasses walked briskly toward a tall steel-and-glass building. She looked up at the looming structure, and then looked right and left. Once inside, she walked to the elevator and pressed the button to go to the thirty-second level. In the elevator, she stood with her head down, looking at the floor, and was the first one to dash out when it stopped. At the end of the foyer, she pushed open a beveled glass door with no sign.

As she entered the room, FBI Chief Gomer welcomed her warmly. His assistant helped her with the coat. The three then engaged in an animated discussion, where Chief Gomer asked questions and the assistant took copious notes for forty minutes or more.

"And those are the only leads he's working on?" the chief asked.

"Yes and the elusive fifth man called Sam he created out of thin air. That's it, unless…" She paused.

"Unless?"

"Well, he's secretive; he doesn't even let me come close to the computer."

"Don't worry, we'll take care of that," the assistant quipped.

"Does he suspect you?" the chief asked Moira, ignoring his assistant's comment.

"He's intuitive but his prejudice exceeds his intuition. He believes estrogen makes women dumb." Moira smiled wryly. "It works all right for me."

"Estrogen?" the assistant asked.

"Prejudice, my dear. Male prejudice works for me," Moira said with a straight face.

"Has he ever been suspicious of you?" the chief asked.

"I think he's suspicious of every human being. At least in that way he's very democratic," Moira said sarcastically, rising from her chair. "It's time for me to go. You know his antennas would go up if I'm late."

Chief Gomer and the assistant escorted Moira to the elevator. Once she was gone, the chief turned to the assistant.

"You think women are dumb?"

"Frankly speaking—" the assistant began to respond.

"Frankly speaking, men who think women are dumb need to explore new clichés." The chief interrupted rudely.

CHAPTER 31

It was a sunny day, a typical California afternoon. The last bell rang, and students were happy to go home for the weekend. Tommy, deep in his thoughts, walked to the gate. Unknown to him, the regular four bullies who frequently ridiculed Tommy waited for him about thirty yards from the gate. They were clad in white karate uniforms with red belts and holding baseball bats.

All four smirked with a resolve to attack Tommy that afternoon. Wielding their baseball bats like swords, they lay in wait for him. One of them held a local newspaper with a large picture of Tommy.

"Puny little show-off." One boy contemptuously threw the newspaper on the ground. Others stepped on it menacingly, grinding their heels on the prominently displayed photo.

The boys saw Tommy walk past the gate. According to plan, the four boys were to walk behind Tommy, keeping a safe distance until they turned the corner, and then they would charge at him with baseball bats.

"Run, Tommy!" Megan came out of nowhere and yelled. Tommy saw the four assailants behind him. He ran in the opposite direction, which took the boys by surprise. Nevertheless, they gave chase, menacingly flailing their baseball bats in the air.

"Tommy, run!" Megan, who was between Tommy and the boys, yelled again and began to run ahead of the charging boys. For Tommy, there was no time to panic. He mustered all his strength and sprinted for dear life.

Tommy ran a good half mile with Megan and his foes behind him. Panting for breath, he came to the end of the field next to the Graywater Reservoir, which was deep and often muddy. Tommy stood at the edge of the stream. It was twenty feet wide and equally deep. There was no way Tommy could swim; besides, he was afraid of water. With his mouth going dry and his heart pounding against his chest, he looked over his shoulder as the boys with baseball bats closed in on him.

Tommy anticipated a beating resulting in serious, bloody injury. The boys slowed their pace and smiled. There was no way Tommy could escape their wrath. Megan looked on helplessly, as she, too had reached the edge of the reservoir.

In that moment, desperate and frantic, Tommy did something he would never do in ordinary circumstances. With his eyes shut and teeth clenched, he jumped into the swift, muddy water and ran. To his own surprise, he simply ran over the gurgling water as if there were an invisible pathway made just for him. Tommy covered the twenty-foot distance in a matter of minutes. Astounded, Megan and the boys watched as Tommy splashed his way across the water as if he were on a wet marble floor.

For a few moments, everyone looked bewildered including Tommy. Then with moans of anguish, the boys turned around, threw their baseball bats on the ground, and ran back as fast as they had come.

"Hey, Tommy, good for you!" Megan stood on the other edge and shouted across the swift river.

"Thanks, Megan," Tommy shouted back across.

"Tommy, if you teach me to walk on water, I promise to marry you."

"Of course," Tommy said excitedly and jumped into the water. Except this time, he disappeared in the water for a few moments and then surfaced, gasping for breath. He barely managed to come up, and when he did, he held onto a mossy stone for dear life. The magic moment had passed like a thought.

"I can't," Tommy said, out of breath and spitting muddy water.

"Sexist," Megan sighed and left.

Spalding was euphoric at having cracked at least a part of the case. Every brain wave Spalding had was on the money, and every step he took paid off. The idea of a fifth man was only a thought until he materialized. It was indeed ingenious, and Spalding thought he had earned the awe of his peers.

Spalding decided his next move would be to take Tommy to a hypnotist and draw out that repressed memory loaded with nearly a hundred million dollars worth of antique jewels. He had located a hypnotist in San Francisco who had a reputation for helping people with substance abuse addictions by autosuggestion. He had also assisted people in ridding themselves of stammering and anger issues. His modus operandi was to put people in a state of light sleep and ask them questions or make autosuggestions. However, when Spalding called with a past-life issue, the hypnotist flatly refused.

"Sir, I help people with issues of anger, stammering, smoking and so forth, the causes of which are hidden in memories of this life. I am not qualified to stir up past-life incidents. I'm not even sure that is possible, although there are others who do it for a living," the hypnotist said.

Spalding offered him twice the normal fee and asked him to educate himself on past-life regressions. He wanted the hypnotist to take Tommy back to his past life when he was Sean Butler and extract whatever information possible. The hypnotist reluctantly agreed and asked for a couple of weeks to prepare.

CHAPTER 32

"I'd love to be hypnotized." Tommy's response surprised Spalding. He did not have to work on the boy at all. Tommy and Spalding met in the park across from the school. It was a chilly, colorless day. All day, the sun played hide-and-seek with the clouds, and finally the dark clouds obscured the sun.

"First I have to apologize to your mother," Spalding reminded Tommy.

"Can we delay it till after we meet the hypnotist?" Tommy was excited.

"Mary, mother of Jesus. Tommy, you always surprise me or am I just getting old"?"

"Will Moira come with us?"

"No."

On the day of the appointment, Spalding picked up Tommy outside the school and drove him to the hypnotist. Before the appointment, they both had an ice cream at the open-air shopping strip close to the hypnotist's house.

"Let's park the car here and walk to his house. It's just around the corner," said Spalding.

The hypnotist's house was a small, quaint cottage isolated from other houses, and it looked like a scene straight from *Wuthering Heights*. The stone walls, covered with ivy, were blackened from years of exposure. Tall grass covered the windows, and smoke was oozing from the chimney. It was a perfect setting for a magic trick or a journey back in time.

Once inside, Tommy and Spalding found themselves in a studio that reminded them of a spooky Hollywood movie. It was semidark with half a dozen candles burning in the middle of the room. The candlestand stood on a dark velvet tablecloth. One wall was painted with the Pangaea supercontinent, before the world divided into the continents we now know. An ancient celestial map lit the ceiling with stars and the Milky Way. The porcelain bust of Tutankhamen, the boy king of Egypt, stared at them from the pedestal.

The hypnotist emerged from behind the red-lace curtain. He was a stocky, weather-beaten middle-aged man with thick glasses. He wore a white silk shirt that was missing buttons on his potbelly. His hair was unkempt, and he walked with the help of a walking stick with a gold-dragon handle.

"Why didn't he hypnotize himself to walk better?" Tommy whispered to Spalding.

"Shh…" Spalding was not interested in the hypnotist's limp.

The shadowy environment was too unfamiliar, and Tommy began to lose his excitement. He did not know what to expect. The idea of hypnotism sounded more exciting than the process itself. He missed his mother.

"Master Thomas Stevenson, please be seated on the couch." The hypnotist took Tommy's jacket and hung it up. Cautiously, Tommy reclined on the couch, which had a deep red velvet cover. Spalding took a chair next to him and flipped open his spiral notebook.

The air was full of suspense for all three.

The hypnotist produced a gold-and-black medallion on a chain from his pocket and dangled it in front of Tommy.

"Master Thomas, please focus on the medallion. You may blink but not remove your gaze from this object," the hypnotist said, dangling the medallion in front of Tommy. The boy, his heart beating against his chest, submitted himself.

"You will go into deep slumber but respond to my questions as if you're awake. You will not remember anything when you wake up. Are you ready, Master Thomas?" the hypnotist asked.

Tommy nodded weakly.

The hypnotist clicked his finger and swung the medallion slowly. Tommy looked nervously at Spalding, and then at the door. If possible, he would dash for the safety of the known.

"Keep your attention on the medallion. Are you sleepy?" the hypnotist asked.

"Hm."Tommy began to feel his eyelids grow heavy.

"Now, go back in time. I want you to grow smaller and smaller."

"Hm."

"You are back in the belly of your mother. Are you there?"

"Ah."

"Now, I want you to go three years back. Are you there?"

"Yes, I am."A very happy response startled Spalding.

"Are you Tommy?"

"No. I'm Sean."

The hypnotist looked triumphantly at Spalding, who was scribbling feverishly.

"Tommy, can you—"

"I'm Sean,"Tommy spoke clearly through closed eyes.

"Sorry, Sean, where are you?"

"At the beach with Mom and Dad. My mother's reading a book, and my father is helping me build a sand castle."

"Now let's go back to your last day on earth. What is your name, and how old are you?"

"Sean. I'm eleven years old,"Tommy's voice had changed. It was thin, and he spoke haltingly.

"Good. What are you doing?"

"We're camping near a lake. I'm with my parents and playing with a dog."

"Great. What is your mother's name?"

"My father is saying to my mother, 'Mary, time for lunch.' Her name is Mary."

The hypnotist and Spalding exchanged glances. Spalding's eyes sparkled. Everything was working. Tommy was in deep regression.

"Do you see some men?"

There was a brief pause.

"Yes, four or five men. They're drinking and very excited."

"Good, Tommy, now what do you see?"

"Who's Tommy?"

"I'm sorry. Sean. What are the men doing now?"

"They are fighting. One man hit another man. The man who was hit is angry. He takes out a knife…"

Spalding felt the rush of blood in his veins. The hypnotist looked pleased. "What happens next?"

"They see my parents watching. They're angry. They curse."

"What happens next?"

145

"Oh no!" Tommy began to breathe heavily.

"What happens now? What do you see, Sean?"

"Oh, no…" Tommy began to heave and choke. His speech was garbled. In deep sleep, he began to pant. Beads of perspiration appeared on his forehead and upper lip.

"Tommy, I mean Sean, don't lose me. Stay with the scene. Do they come for your parents?"

"Ah!" Tommy looked as if he was witnessing something terrible.

"What are they doing, those bad men?"

Tommy's hands reached for his own neck and produced a choking sound. He had stopped talking.

"Tommy, I mean Sean, do you see jewels, a bag or a sack of jewels?" Spalding butted in. The hypnotist looked at him disapprovingly and motioned for him not to interfere.

"Stay with the scene, Sean. What's happening now?" The hypnotist tried to save the trance, but it was too late. Tommy mumbled again; his body heaved as if he was trying to run away. In doing that, he fell off the couch and lay on the carpet staring at the ceiling with an empty gaze. He was definitely not in a trance.

"Cut out the bullshit, Tommy," Spalding yelled. "I paid this dimwit five hundred dollars for this session. Jog your memory, young man. Try and remember what happened."

Tommy continued to stare at the ceiling. Spalding bent down, pulled Tommy up by his shoulders, and shook him.

"C'mon, you asinine brat! You hold the key to a hundred million dollars worth of booty and my future. Think hard, or you'll die again." With that, Spalding sank to the sofa. "My God, I don't believe I said that. Christ, we were so close."

Disoriented, Tommy struggled to his feet and looked around at the inhospitable surroundings. He didn't remember what had happened, but he didn't like the look on either man's face. He needed to get out into the open.

❧

Once outside, Tommy ran a short distance and then slowed down. Even though he didn't remember anything that transpired in the studio, he was glad to be out of the surreal surroundings. He took a deep breath and walked along the shopping strip where they had parked the car.

Suddenly, the sky began to darken. Tommy looked up and saw menacing, black clouds move over the sun. He quickened his pace, but before he knew it, rain poured from the sky. Quickly he took shelter under the awning of a store window and waited for the downpour to end.

While standing under the awning, he felt movement behind him and looked over his shoulder into the shop window. It was a jewelry store. The store employee, holding a box of jewelry, was rearranging sparkling gems on display. He laid out a purple velvet cloth and began to arrange them. Through the glass window, the man smiled at Tommy, who smiled back in acknowledgement.

The associate was distracted for a moment. The box dropped from his hand, and some of the jewelry fell over the purple velvet. He quickly picked up the jewels, arranged them neatly for window display, smiled again at Tommy, and disappeared inside the store.

Tommy felt a warm sensation in his body. In that moment, he became detached from his immediate surroundings. He felt a sensation in his body of a similar scene he may have witnessed earlier. A shiver ran up his spine as he stared at the glittering display through the store window. A scene began to play out in front of him as Tommy stood motionless, facing the jewels on display.

Up on the hill near a lake, a man held his bleeding stomach with one hand and a box in the other and crawled under a parked car. He was trying to hide from a bunch of men who were drinking and arguing. Once under the car, he lay flat on his back and started to tinker with the engine.

The wounded man then moved out from under the car and crawled cautiously toward a van parked nearby. He was not visible to the gang members. The box he was carrying hit a stone and opened, spilling out a bunch of the glittering treasure. The wounded man quickly scooped up the jewels and disappeared inside the van. Next instant, the van started, swerved, and lurched on the road. The other men stopped arguing and dashed toward their car.

"Tommy." Spalding's voice came from behind, and the scene melted into thin air. For a moment, Tommy had difficulty placing himself in the situation. *What am I doing here?* Adjusting his baseball cap, he stepped out from under the awning and looked up at Spalding.

"Sorry I yelled at you, young man." Spalding handed Tommy his jacket.

Tommy nodded and walked with him to the car. He was so engrossed in his thoughts that he did not notice the clear blue sky and the bright sun. There were no clouds as far as the eye could see. The air was crisp and dry, and there was not a drop of water anywhere on the road or in the sky.

CHAPTER 33

"Okay, here's the priority list. First, the apology note I wrote for your mother. Tell me what you think." Spalding pulled out a handwritten note from under the keyboard. They were both at the reporter's home.

"It says: 'Mrs. Stevenson, I am very sorry for what I have done. It was wrong of me to have put your son's life in danger. Greed and ambition can make people do evil things. And I am guilty of both. Please forgive me. Sincerely, Derek Spalding.'" Spalding read out the note to Tommy.

"That should calm her down." Tommy was pleased.

"And now I want to apologize to you again for behaving badly at the hypnotist's. The session was going so well that when you didn't respond to the important question, I lost my cool. Also, I think the hypnotist was inexperienced."

"Or maybe I just clammed up."

"Either way it was my fault. And I want to make up for it. Tell me what I can do for you. Shall we go for a hot fudge sundae?"

"Do you have a gun?" Tommy asked.

"Mary, mother of Jesus. You asked me once before. What will you do with a gun?"

"I just want to see one up close."

"Okay, I would have preferred ice cream, but if you want a gun, I'll show you one." Spalding moved to the huge bookshelf. "Remember the date today; it's your day of initiation."

"When did you buy your first gun?" Tommy asked.

"Just before my second divorce."

"Did you use it?"

"No, I found a good lawyer." Spalding pulled out a voluminous copy of the *Encyclopedia Britannica*. He opened the book to reveal a deep, hollow chamber cut to the size of a small gun. Spalding took out the gun and handed it to Tommy, who was fascinated by the touch of the cold metal.

"This is a German nine-millimeter pistol. So far, I have only used it to test-fire. It has a two-grip back strap for larger or smaller hands. The handle is dark blue. Don't miss the barrel made of pure stainless steel, a real beauty," Spalding explained proudly.

"Cool." Tommy held the small pistol in both hands, feeling the contours.

"And here is my name etched on it." Spalding showed Tommy a small etching on the inside.

"What about bullets?"

"Coming right up, Master Thomas." Spalding darted to the maple buffet near the dining table. He picked up a decorated cut-glass goblet, removed the lid, and scooped out six metal tipped bullets from it.

"Now put them in the gun," Tommy said excitedly.

"At your service, Master Thomas." Spalding fed the bullets into the gun.

"Use it."

"Go stand near the door," Spalding said, taking aim at Tommy, who was about ten feet away from him. "Now say something to get me mad."

"I want a divorce," Tommy said, laughing.

"A divorce? Take this instead," Spalding said angrily, aimed and fired the gun.

Just as he fired, Moira walked in with an armful of files. She collapsed in a heap of files. Tommy's eyes dilated with horror. He gaped in panic. Moira was on the floor, not making any movement. In the hush that followed, Tommy could hear the sound of his heart thumping against his chest.

Mozart's symphony broke the moment of stunned silence as an unruffled Spalding turned on the stereo and poured himself a drink. Moira realized she was not hurt. Spalding winked at Tommy and secretly opened his right hand. All six bullets were still in his palm.

"Is that a real gun?" Moira asked, embarrassed, picking up the files from the floor.

"Nah, it's Tommy's toy." He winked at Tommy again and tossed the empty gun at him.

Later that evening, Spalding drove Tommy home.

"Don't forget to give the note to your mother and tell her I will drop in one day and apologize personally," Spalding said.

"I don't have it," said Tommy.

"Oh, shucks, I forgot the note on the table," Spalding said, groping in his pocket. "Okay, I'll write another one." He pulled the car to the side of the road, produced a notepad from his glove compartment, and quickly scribbled the message

"Here, and I still owe you a hot fudge sundae. Let me know when you want a treat. I'll call you Monday, and remember, mum's the word."

༻✿༺

"Wow," gasped Tommy as he watched images of sparkling jewels on the computer screen.

From the day Tommy had the vision outside the jewelry store, he had become obsessed with the jewels. Some things were beginning to clear up as Tommy collected more information on the stolen treasure. He began to surf the Internet for information on the antique jewels that he now felt connected to.

That stolen treasure from the San Francisco Museum of Art never surfaced anywhere, not even in the underground market. It would be difficult to auction them because of their notoriety and historical value. It was becoming more and more likely that the heist was the work of the Scorpio Gang, whose bodies were recovered along with the two stolen cars. But not all of them were dead. Someone *had* survived, but he did not have the jewels either.

It was likely that perhaps Sean Butler or his parents were the last to witness what happened to the cache of gold and precious stones.

In the investigation of the stolen jewels, Tommy was fascinated by the story behind the gems and ornaments. He was amazed to learn of the legend of the rare historical jewels that had seen imperial regalia, bloodshed, changing monarchies, betrayal, and warfare. He began to write the tale of the amazing and priceless ornaments. A few days later, he was ready with the story for Spalding and Moira.

"Legend has it that in the year 1794, young Napoleon Bonaparte fell in love with a seventeen-year-old silk merchant's daughter named Desiree," Tommy read from his research. He was giving a presentation to a very attentive Spalding and Moira at the reporter's home.

"Napoleon was engaged to her for a year and loved her immensely. But the desire to conquer the world overwhelmed him, and he decided not to marry her. She was, after all, a commoner's daughter. He then fell in love and married the famous Josephine." Tommy paused. Spalding looked admiringly at Tommy, while Moira was in a reflective mood.

"But Desiree had her own destiny. Whether deliberately or by a quirk of fate, she managed to marry a general from Napoleon's army. The general was appointed as an heir of the Swedish royal family. He then traveled to Sweden, and Desiree became Sweden's queen," Tommy read from the sheaf of papers.

"During her courtship with Bonaparte, he had showered Desiree with the most exquisite gems and tiaras, including enormous blue-green sapphires weighing nearly forty carats, rubies, and the Hortensia diamond set in gold. The rare Hortensia diamond was peachy-pink in color and weighed about twenty carats. It was part of the French crown jewels that King Louis XIV purchased from India.

"For nearly two hundred years, Sweden kept that treasure under wraps so as not to embarrass the Swedish royal family, which incidentally was established by Queen Desiree." Tommy sipped his soda while Spalding and Moira waited for him to continue.

"In 1995, Sweden loaned that treasure to the United States for a special exhibition at the San Francisco Museum of Art, from where it is believed the Scorpio Gang allegedly pulled off a successful robbery. As historical artifacts, the jewels are priceless. At the time of the robbery, they were priced at thirty-five million dollars. Today they are estimated to be worth over a hundred million dollars," Tommy finished reading his paper to a very attentive duo.

"And you hold the key to where those jewels may be," Moira said thoughtfully.

"And to the thrilling story that I cracked," Spalding said with a satisfied look.

"And I hope I don't remember where they are. Ever," Tommy said. Everyone laughed, not realizing that Tommy meant every word of it. He knew he was alive as long as he did not remember the whereabouts of those jewels.

CHAPTER 34

"Death be not proud"…" For his English literature assignment, Tommy had to pick the best quotation from an old play. He was alone at home, and Carol was at the hospital on night duty. Leo was resting in the cozy comfort of his master's lap. Aussie sniffed around from time to time, for he was slowly losing his eyesight.

Tommy was thinking about Megan and Johnny. Megan was ready to be his friend again. Johnny was wavering between friendship and jealousy, while Pete was still anxious. Tommy missed the good old days, and he had the recurring thought, *What would have happened if I was not randomly selected to play Sean Butler?*

The phone rang. It was his mom checking on him. After her usual questions, she said, "By the way, you know the young man who visited you the other day, the one in the black Beetle? I forgot how you know him."

"Mom, he wanted to interview me," Tommy lied.

"Oh. He is in the ICU. His girlfriend ditched him, and he tried to kill himself."

"I'm sorry to hear that." His heart missed a beat. As soon as he disconnected the phone, Tommy quickly put on his jacket, went outside, and got on his bike.

He rode as fast as he could down the road illuminated by fluorescent streetlights. It was a cold night, and no one saw him.

Once he was near the hospital, he left his bike on the lawn and ran inside the open door. During night shifts, the staff was practically cut in half. The receptionist, her back to Tommy, was talking on the phone. Tommy bent down, tiptoed by the counter, and then walked briskly to the ICU. His mother had once given him a tour of the hospital, and he remembered his way around.

He checked the names outside and entered the room. Once inside, he closed the door and went up to Chad, who was lying in a bed covered with light-blue sheets. There was a tube sticking out of his mouth, and he had an oxygen mask on his face. The IV slowly dripped glucose into his arm, and the monitor showed a faint pulse. The nurse had just stepped out. Tommy had to act quickly. Softly, he walked to Chad and whispered in his ear.

"Come back, Chad. Death will not end your suffering. It'll only delay completion. If you go now, you'll have to start all over again." He stopped and looked apprehensively at the door. The nurse would be back any moment.

"Don't break the rules of the Universe, Chad. Complete the journey, and things will start to move in the right direction. My friend, you have no choice." Tommy nervously looked at the door as he heard footsteps in the corridor.

"The only permanent thing is change," Tommy said, gently rubbing Chad's palm. A moment later, he noticed movement in Chad's fingers, and the pulse on the monitor picked up speed.

"Cool! Death be not proud"…" With that, he stepped out of the ICU, ran across the hall, and turned the corner. There Tommy saw his mother on duty, walking toward him, reading a file. Tommy prayed she would not see him as he walked stealthily past her and quickly turned a corner. Carol sensed something odd. She looked around but saw no one. Shrugging her shoulders, she entered Chad's room.

"Whew, that was a close shave," Tommy muttered. He picked up his bike and rushed home before his mother called with more instructions. The weeping willows on the side of the road swayed in the cold wind like drunken sailors.

"Let's go watch the movie *Kundan*. It's about the present Dalai Lama," Carol said to Tommy on a Sunday afternoon. "After the movie, we'll have lunch at the new Tibetan restaurant. They're famous for their vegetarian pot stickers."

"Cool!" Tommy was thrilled. "I have an assignment to write a paper on a winner of the Nobel Peace Prize. The Dalai Lama would be perfect."

Tommy enjoyed the precious moments in the movie theater with his mother. They munched on buttered popcorn and drank soda while Tommy was riveted by the story of the Dalai Lama.

About four years after the death of the thirteenth Dalai Lama, as per their tradition, Tibetan men and women from the monastery traveled in search of the reincarnation of His Holiness. The search for the present fourteenth Dalai Lama ended as they came to the house of two-year-old Tenzin Gyatso in a remote village in Tibet.

Tommy was spellbound as the scene unfolded where the two-year-old was asked to select the belongings of the dead Dalai Lama from a group of items. Some did not belong to the expired spiritual guru. Little Tenzin picked out a brass bell, wire glasses, a walking stick with a carved silver handle, a wooden cup, and a crystal necklace. Everything he picked indeed belonged to the thirteenth Dalai Lama. At the end of the spectacle, the search party, made up of village elders from the temple, knelt before the toddler and declared him the fourteenth Dalai Lama, the reincarnation of the thirteenth Dalai Lama.

"What does the term Dalai Lama mean?" whispered Carol.

"In Tibetan, *Dalai* means 'ocean,' and *Lama* means 'spiritual teacher,'" Tommy whispered back.

"That's my boy." Carol squeezed his arm proudly.

They watched the rest of the movie in rapt silence. Tommy was fascinated by the rough and unfriendly terrain of Tibet. The dry, rugged mountains stretched from one end of the vast horizon to another. Tibet was also known as the Roof of the World.

A cold shiver ran through Tommy as the movie screen slowly changed to something very different. Wet, uneven cliffs above a blue lake replaced the desolate mountains of Tibet. Tommy watched in frozen silence as the scene changed to the all-too-familiar topography of San Felipe, California.

A bunch of men laughed and celebrated their successful robbery. They showed each other their tattooed biceps. Drinking, laughing, and backslapping each other, they opened a box that glittered with tiaras, necklaces, and bracelets studded with rare gems. They flipped heavy gold coins in the air and played with the jewels.

Suddenly, one of the men said something, and the guy next to him punched him in the face. He started to bleed. The revelry turned into a brawl. The bleeding man whipped out a knife, and before the others could stop him, he stabbed the man who had punched him. The injured man collapsed to the ground.

A vacationing couple, preparing to sleep in their van, witnessed the scene with horror from an area above the lake. As the brawl continued, the fighting men saw the couple and realized they had seen too much. They chased the two, who ran to their parked van. The couple got in, but the three men quickly caught up with them and overpowered them. There was a brief scuffle, and the men had strangled the man and woman. The men then locked the windows and doors, pulled the handles out, and pushed the van into the lake. A small white-and-brown shaggy dog outside the van barked incessantly.

While this was going on, no one noticed a young boy sleeping in the back of the van under a blanket. As the mayhem continued, the terrorized boy quietly opened the back door and rolled out. He fell on the ground, still in his blanket, and stayed there trembling. As the boy lay on the wet ground, he witnessed an unusual scene.

An injured man, holding his bleeding stomach with one hand and a box with the other, crawled under a dark-colored car with tinted glass windows. Underneath the car, the injured man put the box on the ground and tinkered with something. He then crawled out, still holding his bleeding stomach and the box. The boy saw him, but the rest of the men were distracted by their scuffle with the couple. Then the injured man got into another van and turned the ignition on.

Suddenly a shadow fell across the boy, and he saw a noose lowered in front of him.

The boy screamed, but the noose quickly went around his neck and tightened. A dog barked incessantly and scampered around wildly. The boy chocked.

"You okay, honey?" Carol asked a startled Tommy.

"Yeah!" Tommy whimpered.

On the screen, the Dalai Lama had safely escaped to India.

After the movie, they had the Tibetan meal at the restaurant.

"What part did you enjoy most?" Carol asked.

"The part where the two-year-old was asked to select the belongings of the thirteenth Dalai Lama," Tommy responded with as much normalcy as he could muster.

"I liked the part where Dalai Lama escaped from the Chinese government to India," Carol said.

"Today, the fourteenth Dalai Lama is in exile in India. They are struggling nonviolently to free their country," Tommy added.

On the way back, Tommy did not say anything to his mother. But when they reached home and it was time for them to say good night, Tommy grabbed her arm.

"What's the matter, honey?"

"Mom, can I sleep in your room?" Tommy asked feebly.

"Of course, sweetheart."

Tommy was already in Carol's bed while she brushed her teeth. She came out and got into her bed. She was startled as Tommy rolled over and hugged her tightly.

"Mom, do you believe in reincarnation?"

"I'm confused about it, honey. I think in cultures where they believe in reincarnation, they do have such events."

"Then why do I remember what I remember?"

"I don't know sweetheart, coincidence…maybe."

"You're my mom, and the best in the world, that's no coincidence." Tommy hugged her tightly and rolled over. "Good night, Mom, I love you."

CHAPTER 35

Tommy sipped hot chocolate while Spalding typed on the computer. They were in Spalding's messy living room, and Tommy was narrating the images he experienced in the theater watching *Kundan*.

"How long did the flashback take you? I mean, how much of the movie did you miss?" Spalding asked.

"I didn't time it. The images of the couple, the boy, and the robbers took something like a half hour. But when my attention returned to the screen, it seemed I had missed only a minute of the movie."

"Perhaps time and space as we know don't exist in imagination."

"Perhaps."

"Wow! What a story. Anything else you remember, Tommy, about the injured man with the box?" he asked, typing the last sentence.

Tommy shook his head anxiously. He did not share Spalding's enthusiasm.

"Can you recall how many men were there?"

"I saw four with painted biceps, tattoos, I guess. I did not see the fifth, who strangled the boy…" Tommy said haltingly.

"Tommy, you hold the key to the jewels. None of the four men who died had them. Even Sam, our fifth man, who I think is stalking you, doesn't have them.

If he had those darn jewels, he would have gotten you by now. You'll lead us to him, to the priceless historical jewels, and my salvation."

Tommy was quiet.

"Sorry Son. I didn't mean to be callous. We won't let any harm come to you."

Tommy's response was a sullen silence.

⁂

Spalding was excited. He had spent the whole night painstakingly putting together the pieces of the jigsaw puzzle of the Butler family murders, and a picture had begun to emerge. He felt proud of himself. He had done it without the help of the police or the FBI. The intelligence agency was still groping in the dark because they had no information, and the clues that Tommy was giving were solely the property of Spalding. The fiercely secretive reporter was not sharing this new information with anyone, not even Moira, who was showing signs of frustration.

But he had gained some success, and he felt it was time to include her in the discussion and use her as a sounding board.

"I'll wait for you in the conference room. Bring some coffee for both of us," he said and marched to the conference room.

"Why do you have to put up with his rude behavior?" a female colleague prodded Moira.

"Because…" Moira said belligerently, striding out of the room.

In the conference room, Spalding read from a stack of papers and began to write on the whiteboard.

"You can actually work without music. It must be serious," Moira said lightheartedly.

Spalding ignored her remark and continued to work on his chart.

"Now, listen carefully and tell me if there is a missing piece here." he stood holding a clipboard and a marker. He was ready to piece together the great story of the decade and title it "The Fifth Man."

"According to Tommy's recollections just before he—I mean Sean—was strangled by someone, he saw an injured man crawl under a car with a box in his hands. That was the wounded man Drew for sure, who had loosened the brakes of the Mustang to leak oil. He was still bleeding when he crawled into the black van with the box of jewels and drove off. The four robbers heard the car speed away and noticed the box of jewels was missing.

"They had already killed the Butlers and pushed their van in the lake. One of them strangled the boy, so all witnesses were out of their way. When they saw Drew drive away in the van with the box of jewels, the other four got into the black Mustang and chased Drew. Karadzic and Flynn had to be in the back seat, Tanner was at the wheel, and Sam, our phantom man, was in the front passenger seat."

"Explain the sequence. First you create a phantom fifth man, and then you place him in the front seat," Moira asked disbelievingly.

"It was a two-door Mustang." Spalding ignored the puzzled look on Moira's face. "Flynn and Karadzic were trapped in the back seat; that is how the paramedic found them. Tanner was at the wheel. When the accident happened, Flynn and Karadzic died instantly. Tanner died on his way to the hospital. The passenger seat was empty. There *had* to be a fifth man who managed to roll out just in time before the car plunged into Scarborough ravine."

"Objection. There has been no evidence of the fifth man."

"Objection overruled," Spalding said sourly. "Here's the twist. Drew, bleeding from his stab wound, crashed into a tree. The four robbers chasing him noticed the crash. But their car without brake oil and with loosened nuts went out of control, skidded off the cliff, and plunged into the treacherous ravine. I have a hunch that Sam, in the front passenger seat, was able to roll out just in time. He walked to the crash site where Drew either had died or was dying. At that moment, Sam should have walked away with the jewels, and that would be the end of the story."

"Impressive reconstruction, except for Sam," Moira said, not looking completely convinced. "So our phantom fifth man has the jewels?"

"No, he doesn't."

"He doesn't?"

"That's the missing link. What happened in those moments when Drew took off with the box and Tanner and company gave chase? I'd give my right hand to know what happened."

"That's because you're left-handed. What makes you so sure Sam was the fifth man in the car and got out just before the accident?"

"What's your problem?" Spalding bellowed. "From the moment I brought Sam into the picture, you have developed chronic fatigue syndrome."

"I don't have anything against a man who, I believe, doesn't exist"

Spalding ignored the remark and offered her a cigarette. She shook her head. "I gave up smoking a long time ago."

"My clue is a pack of cigarettes found in the car. The autopsy showed that none of the four burglars had nicotine in their system."

"Objection; it was a stolen car. The cigarettes could belong to anyone," Moira said.

"Objection sustained. That *is* a valid point," Spalding said. "Except my sixth sense says Sam was the smoker." Spalding pulled out the map that Petrocelli had given him and hung it over the board.

"This is an old map of the area where the incident took place nearly twelve years ago," Spalding said, pointing at the map.

"Maps don't make sense to me," Moira said, still looking disinterested.

"Okay, tomorrow let's go check out the scene of the crime," Spalding said, rolling up the map. Moira's lack of interest in his presentation annoyed him.

CHAPTER 36

It was winter; the air was cold, and the sun balmy and radiant. The trees had shed their leaves and looked desolate. The jagged cliffs were wet, and the lake down below looked turbulent.

Spalding had invited Moira and Tommy for coffee and ice cream. But there was another reason for the trip. Spalding wanted to take Tommy to the spot where the Butler family incident had taken place.

"Don't tell Tommy that we're visiting the area of the crime scene," Spalding said to Moira.

"Aye, aye captain," Moira said excitedly.

They picked up Tommy from his home and drove to Blue Haven Lake.

"Master Thomas, do you want a banana split or a hot fudge sundae?" Spalding asked flippantly.

"I'll start with a banana split," Tommy responded happily.

Spalding followed the directions on Petrocelli's map. After walking for five minutes, they came to an elevation on the ridge right above Blue Horizon Lake. They were surprised to see it was not an isolated stretch of land as Petrocelli had described. There was a huge parking area, and ground was paved with black granite tiles.

"Tommy, go buy your favorite ice cream, and we'll have it on the bench in the open. We'll get our coffee." Spalding gave Tommy some money.

"This is where the Butler van was parked." Spalding said to Moira pointing at an area on the map outlined in pencil. "It has to be. The van was facing north when they pulled it out of the lake."

"The bodies of the parents were found on the seats. How did Sean's body get swept away a hundred yards into the lake?" Moira asked.

"Good question. I have a hunch that the burglars strangled the parents and pushed the van down into the lake to give the appearance of an accident. Moments later, one of them found Sean, who had slipped out of the van. He strangled the boy and pushed his body over the cliff into the lake, here." Spalding pointed the spot on the map where it said the police had found Sean's body downstream."

"Your imagination is pretty gruesome." Moira's voice quivered.

The air was still nippy, but the sun was warm on their faces. In silence, both absorbed the possible scenario.

"This is where the murders took place, and this is where the jewels are," Spalding said emphatically. "They have to be here somewhere."

Tommy appeared with a large banana split. He joined the two, placed his ice cream on the bench, and looked around.

"Anything wrong, young man?" Spalding asked as Tommy's expression began to change. He looked confused and restless.

"My shoelaces." Tommy pointed at his untied shoelaces and bent down to tie them. He then reached out and touched the ground.

"Tommy, dear, do you remember anything?" Moira startled him with a question. Tommy pulled back as if there was an electric shock. He looked up at Moira's questioning eyes and panicked.

"No." Abruptly, Tommy turned around and ran to the parking lot. His banana split remained untouched on the bench.

Spalding and Moira exchanged glances.

"I'll take this to the boy. Why don't you go get coffee for both of us," Spalding said, picking up Tommy's banana split.

"Look, Grossman is coming out of the restaurant," Moira said. "I told you we should keep an eye on him. He's following us."

Grossman, wearing a baggy tracksuit, walked out of the restaurant, looked around, checked his watch, and then walked towards the cliffs.

"I don't think he's our man," Spalding said, walking briskly toward the parking lot. "Don't forget the coffee."

Moira cursed softly as she walked to the coffee shop.

⁂

Two days later, Spalding was back at the same spot alone, or so he thought. Spalding walked around the restaurant in a reflective mood. He occasionally stopped, looked around, then scribbled something in a spiral pad. A couple of times he disappeared inside the restaurant.

Moira watched him from inside her car at a distance. She was bored but had to keep an eye on the secretive reporter. Her phone rang.

"Yes, he's just gone inside the restaurant. He's been in and out a couple of times," Moira said, lowering her voice. She was in the last row of the parking lot talking to the FBI chief. "If I see him making a move, I'll call you." she disconnected, waited a few minutes, and stepped out. She walked a few steps toward the restaurant but decided to return to the car.

She hopped back into the driver's seat, shut the door, and immediately jumped out of her skin as she noticed someone in the backseat. Next instant, she felt a cold metal object pressed to her neck.

"Please don't shoot," Moira pleaded.

"Gotcha, byline burglar," Spalding said between his teeth.

"What the hell?" Moira turned around and felt a surge of anger at her own stupidity. Spalding was holding his pen to her neck.

"This is my story, kiddo," he growled.

"I'm doing all the legwork," she protested, feeling relieved.

"You'll be paid for your athletic skills, gofer. Now cut out the BS and drive. I didn't bring my car," he said, sprawling on the backseat.

"How did you get in?"

"I ask the questions. Why are you following me?" Spalding snarled.

A humiliated Moira was searching for an answer when she saw Inspector Petrocelli walking out of the restaurant.

"I followed you because I saw Petrocelli following you," she said, pointing at the police officer.

The reporter frowned thoughtfully.

Spalding fiddled his thumbs. He was on his fourth beer in the bar, the one where he had met the inspector earlier. *Was it coincidence, or is Moira right about Petrocelli?* The thought kept assaulting him.

There had been times when he was suspicious of Petrocelli. Was it just a simple botched case of investigation, or was there more? How could he not have ordered an autopsy on the bodies? It was unlikely that anyone in the police department would make that mistake. According to Petrocelli, it was an emotionally charged atmosphere when they pulled the dead out of the lake. The people of San Felipe had never experienced anything more serious than a bike theft. The police had admitted to their lapse in judgment.

The question that bothered Spalding was just that. Was it deliberate? Would it be prudent to consider Petrocelli a suspect? Was he hiding behind the blue uniform?

He heard a familiar voice and looked up. Petrocelli was at the counter talking to the bartender. Spalding watched him for a few minutes as if for clues, but his mind was a jumble of thoughts. He was appropriately inebriated and sufficiently confident to start a brawl. He gulped his remaining beer in one swig and staggered toward the inspector, who was sober and alone.

"Was it a case of simple incompetence or calculated oversight, thief...I mean, Chief?" Spalding's voice boomed in the bar. Petrocelli turned around and stared at him while other people watched with interest.

For a moment, Petrocelli did not comprehend what the drunken Spalding was insinuating. But as the meaning of those words dawned on him, the police chief's face turned crimson. His nostrils puckered, and his eyes blazed fire. He stepped back, punched Spalding in the face with full force, and left the bar.

"Who took the key to my drawer?" Spalding frantically rummaged through his papers and books strewn on his unkempt desk. Lately, his sixth sense was bordering on paranoia. He felt people were stealing from him or wanting to kidnap Tommy or plunder his notes for clues to the breaking story.

"I saw you putting it in your inner jacket pocket," a colleague said softly.

"Ah, yes, here it is. Sorry folks, midlife crisis—that's all." Spalding held the key.

The staff exchanged glances as Spalding walked to the editor's room.

"Let's capitalize on the new readers. I want you to follow up on other stories; you're spending far too much time on Tommy," said the editor.

"Now, don't say that," Spalding said with a sinking heart. He was aware that if the editor decided, he could be removed from his beat unceremoniously. "This story is beyond Sean Butler or Tommy. Now it is about the murder of a family, a jewelry heist worth millions, and a botched investigation."

"I want quick results."

"I'm on my way out."

"Where?"

"To have a haircut."

"A haircut during work hours?" the editor thundered.

"Sir, they grow during work hours." With that, Spalding left.

Later that day, Spalding and Moira were out to lunch. As they walked down the street of the busy financial district, he kept looking over his shoulder.

"Do you see anyone behind me who looks suspicious?" he whispered to Moira.

"Yes." Moira rolled her eyes.

"Who?"

"Your shadow and hundreds of hungry people."

"Why do I feel threatened?"

"Sense of importance. How about Japanese food today?"

"Good! Japanese discipline and dedication to work is related to their food."

"Really! Who said that?"

"I just did," he said, pointing at a sushi bar.

"Incorrigible."

"What do you have on Sam Doughty? Find out if he was part of the Scorpio Gang."

"I'm still suspicious of Grossman. At least he's real."

"I cannot honor him with the epithet of a suspect. He's a part-time janitor, lives alone in a dump, and he was conned by an eleven-year-old. I don't respect him."

"What about Petrocelli? He did follow you to the restaurant."

"You also followed me. Does that make you a suspect?" Spalding said, touching his black eye. He did not tell Moira about the incident in the bar.

"My sixth sense tells me Petrocelli's not our man," Spalding said reflectively.

"I think there is a world of difference between your sixth sense and my intuition," Moira said as they entered a restaurant. "One day you'll realize you were wrong all along."

"You're right; my sixth sense is driven by testosterone, and your intuition is mixed-up with estrogen. If history is any yardstick, then we men have been right most of the time. Men made every great discovery, including the discovery of America. Let's celebrate manhood with champagne and sushi," Spalding said, moving toward the bar.

CHAPTER 37

I t was late afternoon; there had been a downpour earlier, and the sky was dark. The cemetery was desolate. Chad stood in front of Sean's grave soaking wet. His clerical collar was gone; he was instead wearing a tracksuit. Slowly he unfolded a piece of paper from his pocket. It was a page from the George Washington Elementary School yearbook, from when he and Sean were classmates. It had Sean's picture and a display of his project, the brass belt buckle he had seen Tommy wearing.

"I've decided to be a football player," Chad said softly. "Telling my folks was not as hard as I thought it would be. They understood that there's nothing worse than an unhappy priest."

Chad and Tommy were having sodas and cheeseburgers in a café near the school. Chad looked like he was at peace. The anxiety lines around his forehead were gone, and Tommy saw him smile for the first time.

""I was in the hospital for a week," Chad said.

"What happened?" Tommy pretended to be surprised.

"I was ill and in a coma…and guess who I saw in my dream?" He paused. "Sean. He visited me in my dream. He told me not to worry. I would be okay." He paused again. "I have something for you." From his jacket, he produced and unfolded a paper.

Tommy stared at the picture of Sean and the art display of the Aztec Ouroboros, like the one on his belt. It was the sign of continuity and rebirth. Tommy and Chad both stared at the page and then at each other.

"I'm sorry for being a bully to you," Chad said apologetically.

Tommy had been glued to the computer for several weeks. His intuition told him to be alert. He could feel the urgency in himself and in the atmosphere. He had designed a website, www.TommyTwiceborn.com, where he had invited young boys and girls who had similar experiences.

"Honey, come down," Carol called. It was her day off, and she wanted to spend time with her son. When Tommy stepped into the living room, he noticed a familiar piece of paper in the wastebasket. He pulled it out. It was the apology note from Spalding.

"Tell him I'm not going to press charges. But next time, I'll kill him with my bare hands if he stepped out of line with you," Carol said, pouring herself a glass of wine.

"You're awesome, Mom," Tommy was relieved.

"Now, tell me, are you catching up in algebra?" asked Carol.

"Don't worry, Mom, I won't let you down."

"Give me a hug." She hugged him warmly. "Promise you won't die on me."

"Oh, Mom!" Tommy was startled.

"Because if you do, I'm going with you." She hugged him again. "I may not be the best mother, but you're all I have. I wish I could bring back your dad."

Tommy was quiet for a moment.

"I never did understand climbing the same mountains again and again, even the Himalayas," Carol said.

"It must be hard climbing mountains?" Tommy asked excitedly, and then realized it was the wrong question.

"Living in the face of danger, falling to sudden death; that's not hard," Carol said, releasing her pent-up frustration. "Going to work with a hangover is hard. Getting an old car fixed is hard. Bringing up a child alone is hard."

"I'm no ordinary child, Mom." Tommy hugged his mom again. "Remember, I've done everything twice." Silence followed his response as the meaning of the words dawned on both.

ᴄ❧ᴢ

Carol tossed the laundry in the washing machine. As she emptied all of the pockets, she pulled out a brass buckle from Tommy's belt.

"What's this?" she asked.

"I don't know. It belonged to him," he said.

"Who?"

Tommy remained silent. Carol looked upset as the meaning dawned on her.

"Honey, I get my dose of weird stuff at the hospital," she said, tossing the buckle in the trashcan.

As soon as his mother left the laundry room, Tommy dashed to the trash can, pulled out the buckle, rubbed it clean with his sleeve, and slipped it into his jacket.

Later that day, when Carol was putting the laundered clothes back in Tommy's closet, she saw a piece of paper sticking out from beneath his clothes. It was an old newspaper clipping. She stared at it for some time and sat on the bed looking defeated. It was a snapshot of Sean's parents, Phillip and Mary Butler.

"When will it end?" she sighed. "I miss you, Frank."

ᴄ❧ᴢ

"Hi!" Tommy was taken by surprise as he heard a friendly greeting from Johnny. Megan and Pete were behind him, smiling.

They were in the school dining room, and as usual, Tommy was all by himself for lunch.

"Hi, Johnny." Tommy was not sure if it was for real.

"Tommy, Johnny here wants to apologize to you for his behavior," Megan said.

Tommy was happy, but still reluctant. "Are we friends again?" He was taken aback as Johnny stepped forward and hugged him warmly. A round of applause from the students greeted this spectacle.

The change from one moment to the other was significant. Yet it seemed there had never been any discord between them. The old friends laughed and backslapped each other. They talked nonstop about things that had transpired during their separation. The Furtive Four had so much catching up to do.

Tommy was surprised to learn that Pete had made a scrapbook of all the news clippings of Tommy. Both Pete and Johnny were thrilled to hold the brass buckle with the strange insignia. Johnny, it seemed, could not get enough of it. They were looking forward to see Aussie up close.

"Let's go to the cemetery once more. That's where it all started. Maybe we'll get some new ideas," said Johnny.

"All right," Pete said half-heartedly.

"But we'll hang out at the entrance; I'll bring Leo and Aussie, the odd couple." Tommy sensed reluctance in Pete.

Later that day, the Furtive Four met at the entrance of the cemetery. Megan and Pete were delighted to play with Aussie.

"I feel Aussie is here to protect you," Pete said, playing with Aussie.

"Everything we did was random and yet..." Johnny said.

"It seems there was a divine plot in our random acts," Megan said.

"There's nothing random in life. We were on a mission. We still are," Tommy reflected.

"We never met a real ghost, and I never got to use my BB gun," Johnny said sullenly.

Everyone was silent for a moment before they all burst out laughing. Aussie gave a howl in the direction of the cemetery. Leo stood up on Aussie's back and looked around importantly, wiping his eyes with his long tongue. He looked happy to be part of the reconciliation. The wind picked up speed, and the giant oak trees stood guard above the friends as the leaves rustled and the branches swayed. The Furtive Four looked at each other and smiled. They were not afraid anymore.

"Let's go to my place," Tommy said.

"Hey, Mrs. Stooksberry's going to be the chairman of the parent-teacher' council," Pete said as they walked towards Tommy's house.

"How can she be a chairman; she doesn't shave," Johnny asked gruffly.

"You mean our new chairperson," said Megan.

Tommy was quiet. He had heard that before.

CHAPTER 38

It had been two days since Tommy had reconciled with his old friends. Every day they had been out having sodas and cheeseburgers and making up for lost time. The four talked about everything under the sun, including issues that were hot topics on television.

"Global warming is melting glaciers and our coastlines will change." Pete had done his research.

"We'll be surrounded by water, but fresh water will become scarce," Megan said with sadness.

"The next war could be for water," Pete said.

"I'll finally get to use my BB gun." Johnny was his usual self.

Everyone had a hearty laugh. Tommy enjoyed being with his friends again. But something was troubling him.

It was six in the evening, and Tommy was home, doing his homework. Aussie was snoozing, and Leo was in his dry aquarium. Tommy had just taken his insulin shot and was waiting for his mother's call.

He had been restless since he had made up with his friends. Before he went to bed, he had gone over the events of the last few days and made notes of everything that had transpired since. He had even written down the conversations with his friends, and he went over his notes until his eyes ached and the words began to dance in circles. He then lay on the sofa and dozed off.

"Oh, fudge!" A few minutes of relaxation and the idea came like lightening. He jumped up, alerting Aussie and sending Leo scampering around the room. The thought was clear in his mind. It was there all along, but he was a victim of his conditioning. He quickly dialed Spalding's number.

"Please, God, let him be sober," Tommy prayed.

"Hello, my friend." Spalding was sober at the other end.

"I have something that will blow your mind away," Tommy said excitedly.

"Go ahead, make my day."

Tommy and Spalding talked for a while on the phone. For several minutes, Spalding listened attentively.

"Mary, Mother of God, you're a genius, Tommy. I predict you'll make a great investigative reporter," Spalding was exuberant.

"Genius has nothing to do with it. It's a matter of survival," Tommy said.

After talking to Tommy, Spalding turned on his computer, turned on Mozart, poured himself a drink, and began to search the database of police files once again, this time with a new zeal. The phone rang. It was Moira.

"I'm driving to your house with information on Sam Doughty. Your hunch was right. I think he's the man we're looking for. But he's missing," Moira said excitedly.

"Toss that information in the nearest dumpster," Spalding said coolly.

"What?"

"Toss the file and go home," Spalding said in his inimitable style. "We were on the wrong track all along. I've cracked it finally. Have a good night's sleep. And don't forget to read the headlines tomorrow." Spalding hung up.

❧

Moira had called him from her car. With great uneasiness, she heard the click of the phone disconnecting her call. Angrily she dropped the phone in her bag, pulled over to the side of the road, and paused to think. Several minutes later, she turned the ignition key and slowly drove to a roadside trash can and tossed the file. She then swerved her car in a U-turn, narrowly missing an oncoming car.

"The secretive SOB." She clenched her teeth and drove at breakneck speed.

Spalding worked feverishly at the computer. The loud sounds of Mozart wafted out of his house. He could not believe that the breakthrough came from Tommy. The clues were all there. He scanned the police files of suspects with first names and aliases of Sam. Quickly he selected some and clicked open the files.

He reached for an apple he had been eating, took a bite, and put it back near the keyboard. A drop of blood trickled from the apple onto the plate. The excitement of the new revelation had robbed the reporter of his sixth sense for danger.

Spalding was so engrossed in his work, and the music was so loud, that he did not hear the muffled click of the hummingbird device on his bedroom window. Someone dressed in a black, hooded suit with black gloves had entered his bedroom. The hooded person tiptoed toward the living room, where Spalding was totally immersed in his work.

Spalding's back was to the door. He was downloading a picture of Sam. Sensing he was not alone in the room, Spalding turned and saw the masked person holding a gun. Before Spalding could react, the masked figure pulled the trigger, and Spalding fell to the carpet, bleeding profusely. As the picture of Sam slowly downloaded on the internet, the intruder produced a glittering piece of jewel from inside the hooded suit, lifted the couch cushion, placed it near the hidden brochure, and put the cushion back. The masked figure then slipped the gun in Spalding's left hand and pulled off the mask.

The picture of Sam was fully downloaded, and it was the image of a young Moira. Her full name, Moira Allen Shaughnessy, read backward as SAM, her alias. Spalding's attacker, Moira, who had taken off her hood, quickly punched a number on her cell phone. Spalding's cell phone, sitting near the keyboard, buzzed a couple of times before the call went to voice mail.

"Spalding, I've checked on Sam Doughty. I have the details. I am heading home; call me in a half hour." She left a message while looking at the fallen Spalding. Lightly she kicked his face out of her way as she sat in his chair and deleted the picture he had just downloaded.

In the FBI office, the assistant was monitoring Spalding's computer remotely. He saw a message: Downloading Picture on Host Computer. Back in Spalding's house, Moira quickly deleted his files.

"Estrogen, my dead partner, gives me an edge when it comes to consistency, detail, and obvious vulnerability," she said with contempt to Spalding's lifeless form. She stuck a business card in his collection of cards.

"Besides, it's a natural shield against osteoporosis, heart attack, and in some cases unnatural death." She walked up to the front door, locked it from inside, and put the chain on it, making sure it did not look like a break-in. From her pocket, she pulled out the note to Tommy's mother written in Spalding's handwriting, and placed it near his computer. She took one last look at the room. Everything looked fine and normal. She was wearing gloves and had been careful not to move anything.

Moira entered the bedroom, walked to the window, and climbed out the way she had come in. Once outside, she closed the latch with the help of the secret hummingbird device. Then she firmly yanked and dislodged the contraption.

"Spalding, where are you? Call me." While driving home, she left another message for Spalding.

"Inspector Petrocelli, have you heard from Spalding lately?" Moira called the inspector.

"No, he's probably in hell," Petrocelli said, hanging up.

"For once, you're right." Moira, aka Sam, smiled to herself.

On her way home, she tossed the hummingbird feeder in a garbage can.

CHAPTER 39

Driving home, Moira remembered a scene from twelve years ago.
The four men and Moira were exhilarated at the stunning victory of their jewelry heist. Tanner wanted to take his partner-in-crime and girlfriend, Moira, home and lie low for a while since the police would be out looking for them. Drew insisted they celebrate. Flynn suggested they go to Blue Haven Lake since it was deserted at night, and Karadzic agreed they all needed to chill out. Along with the box of jewels, the car trunk was filled with cold beer.

All five members of the Scorpio Gang drove to Blue Haven Lake in a stolen van and a stolen black Mustang. They parked right above the ridge where no one could see them. They brought out the cold beers and opened the box of jewels. They drank, laughed, and backslapped each other, admiring the glittering loot.

Soon the revelry turned into a brawl. Tanner advised them to keep their voices down, especially Drew, who was drunk and loud. Insulted, Drew punched Tanner in the face with full force. Next instant, Tanner, bleeding from his nose, whipped out a knife from his pocket and stabbed Drew before anyone could stop him. It was sudden, and everyone was stunned. Before the gang members could take care of the injured man, they heard a muffled cry and saw a man and women up on the ridge watching the scene.

The frightened couple, who was camping in that area, ran to their van. But Tanner, Flynn, and Karadzic caught up with them. They opened the doors of the van and grappled with the couple. After a short struggle, the Butlers were overpowered. The couple had witnessed them with the stolen jewels and Tanner stabbing Drew. That could be a death knell for the Scorpio Gang. The three gang members strangled Mary and Philip, propped them in their seats, fastened their seat belts, pulled the handles out of the doors, shut the doors, and pushed the vehicle into the lake.

Moira, who stood guard outside, noticed a frightened boy drop out of the back of the van. The boy was trembling with fear. He had witnessed the murder of his parents. A white, shaggy dog barked relentlessly nearby. Moira pulled her scarf from her neck, rolled it into a noose, and walked up to the boy. Standing behind him, she lowered the scarf and strung it across the unsuspecting boy's neck.

She dragged the lifeless body of the boy in the lake. Just then, the four members of the Scorpio Gang heard the engine of a car. It was Drew, driving away in the van. Karadzic, Flynn, Tanner, and Moira piled into the two-door black Mustang and chased Drew, who had taken the box of jewels.

Drunk and angry, they cursed at Drew. Tanner was at the wheel, with Moira in the front passenger seat. Flynn and Karadzic were in the back seat. Soon they saw the taillights of the car they were chasing on the winding road and knew that Drew could not stay behind the wheel too long because of his serious injury. At the next bend, they noticed the hazard lights of the car about a mile ahead. Drew's van had crashed into a tree. Tanner laughed and the others joined him. They were happy the booty would be divided four ways instead of five.

From the front passenger seat of the black Mustang, Moira noticed the flashing brake light on the dashboard. She knew right away the brakes were loose, and they may not be able to manage the next winding turn. They were all in danger if she did not act fast. She made a split-second decision. She could own all of the jewels if none of them were alive. She took out a pack of cigarettes from her jacket, pulled a cigarette out, and then placed the pack under the dashboard to hide the flashing light. She was the only smoker in the car.

She stared at a sharp bend ahead as Tanner, a little puzzled, noticed her reaching for the door handle. The car, with its damaged brakes, went out of control as Tanner neared the sharp bend. He pumped the brakes, but they had failed. Flynn and Karadzic were trapped in the back seat. Moira opened the door and rolled out onto the side of the mountain just before the black Mustang veered out of control and plunged into the Scottsridge Ravine.

"Sam..." was all Tanner said before he, along with three members of the Scorpio Gang, went hurtling down the dangerous ravine.

Moira watched the car plunge to the bottom of the ravine and knew right away that there were no survivors. She ran at breakneck speed to the crashed van. She found Drew dead at the wheel. She could not believe her luck. She was the sole owner of the thirty-five-million-dollar cache.

Excitedly, she searched the van for the jewel box but found only one piece. Puzzled, she searched again, but there was nothing. She could hear the sound of the police siren in the distance.

She pocketed the lone jewel, threw a burning matchstick on the spilled gasoline, and walked away quickly into the wilderness as flames leapt out of the van.

Back in the present, her train of thought ended as she reached her apartment building. She dialed her phone.

"Spalding, I'm still waiting for your call."

CHAPTER 40

S palding's house and the surrounding area were crawling with police, FBI officers, plain-clothes detectives, and paramedics. The police had stretched yellow tape around the house. The sleepy town of San Felipe buzzed with the news of the alleged suicide of the maverick reporter.

Spalding's body was wheeled out on a stretcher and taken away in an ambulance. Inside Spalding's house, forensic investigators collected evidence.

"Check the exits," Petrocelli ordered his assistant.

"I've checked; all the doors and windows are locked from the inside. There's no forced entry here," the assistant responded. Moira smiled to herself.

The forensic inspector was precisely checking everything in Spalding's bedroom. Moira was with him. She looked at the window through which she had come in the previous night, and her heart sank. The latch was slightly open. When she had disconnected the hummingbird feeder from the latch, it may not have closed properly. With a surge of adrenaline, she looked at the forensic investigator. He was busy dusting the bedside table to collect fingerprints, and his back was to her.

Moira could not take a chance with the evidence she had left. Slowly she pulled out a pencil stuck above her ear and stealthily moved to the open latch. She looked over her shoulder. The inspector was engrossed in his work, but she had to act fast. Slowly, with a pounding heart, she casually moved and stood in front of the latch. With one quick flick of the pencil, she turned the latch into a closed position.

"Did you find anything?" the inspector's voice pierced the loud silence.

"I thought this window was open, but it's latched, see." She pointed at the closed window. *Did he see me in the act?* she thought nervously. It seemed he did not, for he resumed his work.

In the living room, Petrocelli and the detectives were monitoring the collection of evidence. They tried to access Spalding's files on the computer. They had been corrupted when they were deleted. The inspector looked at the note addressed to Tommy's mother. He read the content of the message. The note was stuck on the computer screen in full view.

"Did you find anything in the bedroom?" the FBI chief asked the forensic specialist.

"Nothing. Everything's in order," the inspector replied, and Moira let out a sigh of relief.

In that moment, something very unusual happened, and excitement filled the room. An officer lifted the sofa cushion and found a piece of stolen jewelry and the twelve-year-old brochure from the San Francisco Museum of Art. They examined the jewel in disbelief. It matched the picture in the old brochure. Everyone was stunned. It seemed like someone had sucked the oxygen out of the room.

"Mary, mother of God," Petrocelli said in Spalding's style. "I've never had this kind of experience in my life. So he was the fifth man of the Scorpio Gang."

"Does he have a tattoo?" the FBI chief asked in total disbelief.

"He often talked about new technology to remove tattoos," Moira interjected quickly.

"Here it is." An officer flipping through the card deck picked out a card. "It says 'Tattoo Removal Specialist.'"

No one noticed Moira looking pleased.

"If not for the note and the gun in his hand, I wouldn't believe it to be a suicide," Petrocelli said with a sigh. "But a man who can marry the same woman twice can do anything," he said, dropping the gun in a plastic bag. "And to think he accused me of deliberately messing up the investigation," Petrocelli continued with a strain of anger.

Tommy, devastated and teary-eyed, stood under the willow tree with his friends across from Spalding's house. He had seen Moira walk somberly into the house. He felt sorry for her.

"Spalding is dead because of me," Tommy repeated. Spalding and Tommy had become friends. There were times Tommy looked for his missing father in the eccentric reporter.

Tommy also knew that what looked like suicide was murder. But no one should know about it, definitely not his friends or his mother. He could not endanger their lives. Last night when he gave the final clue to Spalding, the reporter was beside himself with excitement. He had said that was the most glorious moment of his life. And the next morning, he was found dead, allegedly by committing suicide.

"Now only I know the last clue, and I mustn't tell anyone," Tommy muttered to himself.

"Did you say something, Tommy?" Megan asked.

"I want to be alone." He sprinted home, terrified and in turmoil.

I was the last person who called the reporter with the idea that the elusive fifth man was likely a woman, a point we never looked into, Tommy thought.

☙❧

Tommy kept quiet when Petrocelli and the FBI questioned him at length about his phone conversation with Spalding the night before the tragedy. Confused and in turmoil he decided not to say a word about the clue to anyone. He told the police interrogators he had simply called Spalding to touch base. They had talked for barely two minutes. There was nothing new, and Spalding did not mention anything. Tommy had saved his skin for now, and they did not suspect anything.

Moira had a perfect story. She had called Spalding from her car, and he told her to come over. When she reached his house, he would not open the door even though she could see the lights and hear the music. She called from outside and left a message, thinking he might have gone for a walk. On her way home, she left several messages. Finally, she called Inspector Petrocelli.

Later, Moira called Tommy and asked how he was.

"I'm very sorry about Spalding. I always thought he was strange," she said. "But even I did not imagine he could stoop so low. Remember, I'm here for you. If there's anything, talk to me first," Moira told the vulnerable boy.

"You're the only one I can trust," Tommy replied. He was tempted to take Moira into confidence but decided against it to protect her. He was surprised that even she would buy into the suicide theory.

CHAPTER 41

The next few days were frenzied. The local newspapers, TV, and radio stations were buzzing with the peculiar suicide of a reporter who was now being called a deeply disturbed pathological killer and burglar rolled into one. They said he had a severe case of multiple personality disorder. Reporters said he was a maverick who successfully created the elusive fifth man of the Scorpio Gang and then killed himself. But there were many skeptics, like his editor, who said it could not be a suicide. The incredible case was still under investigation.

Carol was devastated at the thought that a killer had been so close to her son. Tommy could not do anything to allay her doubts. She was glad Spalding was out of their lives. Her level of fear had elevated to a point where she had told the hospital she would not work the night shift no matter what.

Tommy could not divulge to his mother his suspicion that someone had killed Spalding. He thought she would have a nervous breakdown if he did.

It was somehow fitting to watch the anchor of the Sunday magazine TV show dedicate the whole hour to the story of Spalding. Tommy watched the program with moist eyes. He knew how passionately Spalding wanted to be the TV anchor.

Tommy had become a celebrity, which was something he did not enjoy. He knew that the story was far from over, and the truth was yet to be unearthed. He was going to be interviewed on the next week's TV magazine show, along with Moira. They were doing a story on Tommy, his past-life recollections, and the extraordinary tale of reincarnation. Carol had allowed it as long as it was the last public appearance of her son.

⊰⊱

It was a cold Sunday afternoon, and the show would be telecast live.

The cloud of Spalding's death had not completely cleared. The investigation was on, and many questions remained unanswered.

Tommy and Carol were going to the studio. His friends Johnny, Pete, and Megan were invited to be part of the studio audience. The program was even going to feature Leo and Aussie. Both had played an incredible role in Tommy's unbelievable story.

On the day of the show, Tommy's mother and friends took their seats in the fully packed studio auditorium. Several security guards in uniform and plain clothes insured the studio's full protection. Inspector Petrocelli was there with his subordinates. Surveillance cameras were installed everywhere. The air was thick with excitement and anticipation.

Tommy and Moira waited in the makeup room to be called on stage. After the makeup man left, Moira and Tommy sat facing each other in awkward silence. The newspaper on the center table had a bold headline.

Spalding's Alleged Suicide.
Was He The Fifth Man?

Tommy looked gloomy as he rubbed the brass buckle he carried with him. He desperately wanted to talk to someone. There was a tenuous calm between the two.

"I know you must be disappointed with Spalding. But try to forget him. He was obviously not worthy of your loyalty." Moira, sensing his unease, moved close to him and held his hand.

"That's not true," Tommy blurted angrily.

"Tommy, dear, is there something I don't know?" Moira was taken aback.

"I have a secret I'm afraid to tell anyone." Tommy could not contain his resolve anymore.

"What secret, Tommy?" she asked softly.

"The last time I talked to Spalding, I told him we were on the wrong track, that Sam was likely a woman. I gave him that clue." Tommy whispered, even though there was no one in the makeup room.

"You gave him the clue." Moira repeated.

"Yes."

"And who gave *you* that clue?" Moira asked gingerly.

"You did."

"I gave you that clue?"

"Yes. Remember how you and Spalding would argue about the existence of the fifth man? I noticed you always said fifth entity or fifth person. You never said fifth man. The other day, my friends said something about Mrs. Stooksberry, our teacher, becoming a chairperson not chairman. And the clue fell into place."

"And…?"

"It all came back to me. It was then I got the idea that Sam was most likely a woman. I was not sure if I was right at first, but now I know I was right because Spalding is dead. He must have told someone right after he talked to me."

"Tommy, do you remember the fifth person?"

"No, I don't remember anything. As for Spalding, it was not a suicide. He was killed. That was not his gun," Tommy said innocently.

"What do you mean, not his gun?"

"He had a real gun with his name etched on it. He got it before his second divorce. But he never used it because he found a good lawyer."

"Where is the gun, Tommy?"

"I have it. But I didn't take the bullets."

"Yeah"…"

"It's hidden under my mattress. I didn't mean to steal; I took it home just for a few days. I was going to put it back. Promise you won't tell anyone?" he pleaded.

"You can trust me. How did you get it?" Moira said, hiding her excitement.

"There is a secret way to get into his house. It's a hummingbird lock no one knows about. Spalding would use it when he was locked out. That's how the killer must have got in. I'm sure of that. I was going to go into the house the same way and put the gun back." Tommy looked relieved after getting everything off his chest.

"Anything else, Tommy?" Moira asked flatly.

"The note they found on him was not a suicide note. It was an apology note he wrote to my mother; he misplaced it and wrote another one. Look, it's exactly the same." He pulled out a crumpled, handwritten note by Spalding, addressed to his mother and placed it next to the newspaper picture of the note found near his body. They were same.

The two stared at each other. Moira sat in menacing silence, and Tommy was unaware of the storm he had stirred up. They were startled when the security guard opened the door of the makeup room.

"You need to come with me, young man," the security guard said and pointed at Moira before he exited the door. "And you're next, ma'am."

Moira smiled at the guard, hugged Tommy, and caressed his head and neck.

"I think Sam is alive. I can feel death around me." Tommy shuddered.

"Tommy, I don't want you to mention this to anyone. Stay close to me. Let's not alarm the killer. Believe me, everything will be all right," she said, looking in his eyes.

"Do you think I'll live to see my twelfth birthday next month?" Tommy looked vulnerable, and he was still whispering.

"You bet. Is there anything else you remember? The jewels?"

"No. And I know I'm alive as long as I don't remember the jewels." Tommy was quiet momentarily. "But if I do, you'll be the first one to know."

"Promise you won't tell anyone." Moira squeezed his hand warmly.

"I promise." Tommy was glad he finally had a confidant.

The security guard escorted Tommy, Aussie, and Leo to the studio.

"Young man, your mom wants you to take your insulin shot before you go on stage."

"Oh, fudge! I left the pouch on the sofa. I'll be back in a jiffy." Tommy dashed back to the makeup room.

He opened the makeup room door, darted in the room, and picked up the pouch from the sofa. Moira was changing into the blouse she would wear for the interview. As Tommy ran out, he noticed a scorpion tattoo with a red stinger, visible just above her right breast.

CHAPTER 42

As Tommy walked down the hallway toward the auditorium escorted by the security guard, he realized his universe had changed in a matter of seconds. He had entered the makeup room without knocking and had seen a sight that took his breath away: the fifth member of the Scorpion Gang.

Tommy walked to the studio, but the world around him began to collapse. With his heart pounding against his chest and his mouth dry like sandpaper, he realized that Moira was Sam. The missing pieces of the giant jigsaw began to fall into place with such speed that he was speechless. According to the phone records, she was the one who had called Spalding immediately after Tommy had spoken to Spalding that night. She was the one who had visited him; she must have known about the hummingbird lock.

Moira Allen Shaughnessy read backward was SAM. She was the one who was following Tommy outside his school. She was the one who spied on him in his own home. She was the one diverting Spalding's attention away from any fifth member of the Scorpio Gang. She was persuading him to investigate Grossman and Sam Doughty instead.

A chill ran up his spine. Spalding must have told her that he had the final clue about the identity of the fifth man. She had killed Spalding. And a few minutes ago, he had opened his heart and confided everything to her. He had walked right into the murderer's den.

He turned his head to look back. Moira, aka Sam, was in the doorway smiling and waving at him. Tommy stared at her with horror in his eyes. She looked confused for a moment. Next instant, the truth dawned on her. From the look on his face, she knew that he knew.

They were both aware that the moment of truth had arrived.

The security guard held Tommy's hand and led him to the studio full of lights and whirring cameras. Tommy held Aussie's leash while Leo stood majestically on Aussie's back.

It was a grand entry. The audience exploded in applause as Tommy entered the stage with trembling legs and took his place on the chair next to the TV host. The host was the most popular anchor, and the ratings of the show were expected to increase sharply. He was glib and handsome with a shock of blond hair and blue-gray eyes.

"Good day, America," the host said to begin the program. "Today we have the most exciting program for you, so stay away from that remote. Among the guests, we have the incredible Thomas Stevenson, also known as Tommy. He has an extraordinary story of past-life recollection, some of which has been verified. We are also going to talk about the sensational suicide of Derek Spalding, the veteran reporter. I stand corrected; it is an alleged suicide, for the investigation is still under way. Accompanying us today is a parapsychologist, Dr. Edward Kipling, who will tell us about paranormal phenomena, past-life memory, déjà vu, and reincarnation." The host paused. "But first, the weather."

Back in the makeup room, Moira was thinking fast and furious. The look on Tommy's face said it all. He knew her identity, and at that very moment, he was sitting in front of an audience of three hundred people and being watched by millions live on the air. She looked up. Hanging on the wall was a huge picture of John Wayne, the all-American cowboy, dressed as a sheriff. She stood up decisively. A smiling security guard appeared at the door. He had come to escort her. She smiled and chatted with him as they walked toward the auditorium.

❧

In the auditorium on the stage, under the glare of lights and whirring cameras, Tommy, the other guests, and the host were seated. The auditorium was relatively dark. The audience listened in rapt attention. Carol smiled at Tommy from the front row, and he smiled back weakly. His mother did not know that Tommy's life was in extreme danger. Tommy looked at Megan, Pete, and Johnny in the row behind his mom.

"Dr. Kipling, tell us about reincarnation and past-life recollections," the host began.

"Well, in Eastern philosophy, birth is not the beginning, and death is not the end. The body is a vehicle that helps us work out our deepest desires and fulfill our karma," the parapsychologist replied.

"Tommy, it is incredible that you remember your past life," the host began. "But more incredible that you solved your own murder. You say events in this life triggered memories of your past life when you were Sean Butler. Tell us more."

Tommy noticed Moira standing in the wings, close to the security guard.

"It also means I could be killed before my twelfth birthday, which is next month. Just like it happened twelve years ago," Tommy said, staring at Moira.

"Oh, c'mon, Tommy, Spalding, the suspected fifth man, is dead," the host said exuberantly. "You're among friends and you have airtight security here. The question is, where are the jewels worth a hundred million dollars? That remains a mystery even now."

Tommy noticed Moira fidget.

"Spalding was not Sam. It was not a suicide. He was killed. Sam is here in the studio."

"Sam's here. The fifth man is here. You know him, Tommy?" the host asked somberly.

The audience became restless; Carol looked ashen. Megan and Pete were alarmed.

"I miss my BB gun," Johnny complained.

Tommy looked at Moira, but she was gone. The security guard was still there, but Tommy noticed something odd about him. Suddenly Tommy felt very cold, just like he had felt in the cemetery when he was selected to play Sean Butler. He opened his sweaty palm and noticed a drop of blood. He shuddered as the feeling of imminent death crawled upon him. He looked at the security guard again, and this time he noticed what was strange. The guard was unaware that his gun holster was empty. The distraught boy stood up and walked up to center stage. He looked above the audience and said loudly.

"Sam, I beg you, give yourself up," he pleaded to an area of darkness beyond the lights. "Sam, you've killed me once. Don't do it again, please."

"Sam is up there? Where? I don't see anyone." The confused host sprang to his feet.

"Sam, you have the choice to break the cycle," Tommy yelled above the audience.

Unknown to anyone, Aussie and Leo had left the stage. Aussie scurried through the hallway and climbed the stairs to the dark balcony. There was certainty in his gait, as if he had recognized someone from the past.

Up above the audience, hidden in the dark balcony behind the big lights, Moira was sitting with a gun pointing at Tommy. Anxiety and dangerous intent contorted her face. She was thinking of her next move. If she killed Tommy, she could at least save herself since no one knew her identity. Even Tommy had not disclosed it.

Down in the auditorium, people were looking up but could not see anything. They, however, heard the sound of the security guards going up the stairs.

"Sam, I forgive you for killing me in the past." Tommy's troubled voice rumbled through the microphone attached to his collar. Carol sprang to her feet.

Moira, still pointing the gun at Tommy, suddenly screamed. Leo had found his way up to the muzzle of the gun. Moira found herself staring into the bulging eyes of the gecko, who was characteristically wiping them with his long tongue as he stood regally on the gun. A panicked Moira pulled the trigger, not once but twice, and ran off the balcony. Aussie was on her heels, growling.

The two shots hit Tommy, and he fell in a pool of blood. His mother, who was about to climb onto the stage, froze as she watched her son collapse.

There was total chaos in the audience. The security guards had reached the balcony and found no one there. They did not know who they were after. Aussie, the only one besides Tommy who knew Sam's identity, ran toward the makeup room. That was where Moira was headed. The emergency exit in that room was her only way out.

Before Moira reached the emergency exit, she pointed the gun at Aussie and pulled the trigger. Aussie, who had already lunged for her, fell on her, bleeding. The gun slipped from Moira's hand. The security guard entered the makeup room and picked up the gun.

"Don't move." He pointed the gun at Moira as she lay under the bleeding dog. Underneath her torn blouse, the scorpion tattoo was visible.

Back in the auditorium, there was total mayhem. Carol had fainted. Megan, Pete, and Johnny wanted to stay close to Tommy, but the paramedics quickly moved the bleeding boy to the ambulance.

There was one question on everyone's mind: will Tommy live to celebrate his birthday next month?'

CHAPTER 43

Tommy had been in the critical ward for forty-eight hours. He lay on the hospital bed with tubes attached to his nose and mouth. An IV hung over his left shoulder. An oxygen mask covered his face. His upper body was wrapped in bandages. The pulse monitor showed a low but steady movement.

In the waiting room, Johnny, Megan, and Pete prayed for their friend. Chad had been on his knees in the church praying. He repeated the message Tommy, as Sean, had told him when he was in a coma. "You've unfinished business here in this world, my friend. Come back. Now is not the time to leave."

Carol paced restlessly as Inspector Petrocelli tried to calm her down. He brought her a cup of coffee; she could not drink more than a sip. Sitting on the edge of the chair, holding her face in both hands, she rocked back and forth.

"Please, God, let my son live. Please," she repeated as if in a trance.

In the meantime, Petrocelli mulled over the recent events. Even though Spalding's death was still being treated as a suicide, the inspector was entertaining the possibility it could be murder. Spalding loved life and liquor too much to go so soon. If he was not willing to kick the habit, he was unlikely to kick the bucket voluntarily.

And then the events at the live TV studio changed the whole scenario. The bizarre episode in full view of millions of viewers left everyone shocked. The newspapers buzzed with stories of Tommy. The TV channels could not stop talking about the boy and the fantastic case of reincarnation. Petrocelli smiled to himself. He had been absolved of his error. The focus was on the FBI, especially Chief Gomer, who had used Moira as an informant. The fact that Moira was the elusive fifth man, Sam, came as a jolt to them.

The police and the FBI were even, each with a botched case.

Moira, aka Sam, had confessed to all the criminal charges. She was the youngest member of the Scorpio Gang and the only woman. Spalding's research had revealed the skills of the other members. Moira, aka Sam, was an aspiring architect. She had helped the gang with the entry and alleyways of the San Francisco Museum of Fine Art. No one in the gang had a prior criminal record, which helped them organize themselves without any suspicion. Tanner had insisted they all get tattoos on their left arms. Moira decided she would get it on her breast instead.

When the Scorpio Gang had successfully pulled off the robbery at the Museum of Fine Arts, they were stunned by their own success. Everything had worked according to plan. They were on their way to becoming rich overnight. But they had not taken the human factor into planning.

"We never expected that emotions would get out of control and we would lose everything," Moira told the police in her confession.

"Tanner was my boyfriend. But Drew liked me too and became jealous of Tanner. I was not interested in either. I had planned to steal Tanner's share and disappear." Moira's confession surprised everyone.

But even Moira did not know where the jewels were. She was certain that Drew, though injured, had carried the box with him. But the valuables were not found on him, and their whereabouts are still a mystery. She was sent to the county prison to await trial.

"Mrs. Stevenson."

'The doctor's entry interrupted Petrocelli's train of thought. Carol, pale and anguished, sprang to her feet and looked expectantly at the doctor. Petrocelli stood beside her and waited for the news. Was the boy going to make it or...?

"Mrs. Stevenson," the doctor said with a smile. "I've good news. Tommy's out of danger. He's going to be all right."

Carol, who had not slept a wink in the last forty-eight hours, collapsed on the floor crying with relief. "Thank you! Thank you, doctor, for saving my son's life."

"We'll keep him for four or five days, and then he should be ready to go home," the doctor said reassuringly.

"Thank God the killer missed the heart," Petrocelli said to the doctor.

"Oh no, the bullet was aimed for the heart," the doctor said. "This saved your son." The doctor produced a shiny object from his pocket.

It was the thick brass buckle in the shape of a snake biting its own tail, the symbol of life and rebirth. Both Carol and Petrocelli stared at it in disbelief as the doctor handed it to Carol. She touched the sharp little depression of the bullet right in the middle where it had bent.

"It was in Tommy's shirt pocket when the shot was fired. If it had not been there..." The doctor stopped and then continued. "The other bullet went above his heart and he lost a lot of blood, but we have fixed that. You have a fine boy, Mrs. Stevenson. You should be proud of him." With those comforting words, the doctor shook hands with Carol and Petrocelli and turned around to leave the room.

"And by the way, you should make preparations for his twelfth birthday," the doctor said as he finally left the waiting area.

In total silence, Carol and Inspector Petrocelli stared at each other and then at the brass buckle.

CHAPTER 44

Three weeks later, on a Sunday, Carol and a healthy Tommy went to the cemetery to pay their respects to the Butler family. Aussie was buried next to Sean. At Sean's grave, Carol kissed the brass buckle and placed it on the granite stone. She trembled with unease, remembering the day she had thrown it in the trash can.

Tommy and Carol placed freshly cut roses on the graves, said their prayers, and looked at each other with moist, smiling eyes. Carol gave Tommy a hug and asked him how he would like to celebrate his birthday.

"Anyway you want, Mom."

"I have news for you. I think we'll have to rent the community hall. Spalding's editor wants to organize the event. They want to celebrate your birthday and honor the memory of Derek Spalding. They've invited everyone from your school and from the press."

Wow!" was all Tommy could utter. He was overwhelmed.

"It's a nice day. Shall we stroll near the lake and have ice cream?" Carol asked.

"Your wish is my command," Tommy said with a sweeping bow. They both laughed as they walked to the car.

They did not know that the powers that be had decided to double their happiness.

The lake area was full of people, and the California sun was out in full glory. Some people were savoring the warm sun, while others were cycling or playing Frisbee. Carol told Tommy to wait on a bench as she walked toward an ice-cream vendor.

Tommy looked at the clear sky, the green hills, and the blue lake, and he was grateful to be alive and well. His wounds had healed, and he would be going back to school.

He noticed a newspaper on the bench. The headlines were still screaming about him.

Where Are The Priceless Jewels?

Tommy turned the paper over. He was sick and tired of the whole business. He did not want to think about those ill-fated jewels that had seen so much history and were still not fading into oblivion.

He missed Spalding. He and Carol had watched the Sunday evening magazine show dedicated to Spalding with teary eyes. The maverick reporter could not host the show, but he was there in spirit. A blow-up of Spalding stood in the background as the host talked about the dedicated reporter who had become obsessed with Tommy's story. He had kept the town and his readers riveted with his meticulous and insightful reporting.

Tommy sat on a bench facing the cliffs on the other side of the lake. He was in deep thought until a boy on the cliff opposite where he was sitting distracted him. The little boy accidently dropped his box of toys. The box opened, and the items inside fell into the lake one by one. Tommy, waiting for his mother to bring him ice cream, had his last episode of déjà vu.

❧

As Sean's killer was overpowering him, the boy witnessed Drew crawl under the van holding his bleeding stomach with one hand and the box of jewels with the other. Drew had altered the brakes on the Mustang. As he dragged his injured body to the van, he lost his grip on the box of jewels. He tried to grab it, but the valuable pieces fell into the lake one by one. Drew managed to grab one piece of jewels, before he crawled into the van. With that last scene, the fascinating flashback was over.

Tommy stared at the part of the lake where he now remembered the box and the contents had dropped. He walked to the edge and gazed deeply into the water. An image of what might be at the bottom of the lake began to take shape in his mind.

He knew the rare historical jewels were underneath the clay, mud, mossy stones, fish, and weeds. They were grimy and muddy, rusted beyond recognition, barely distinguishable from the stones and pebbles, with fish for company. None of the treasure was visible to the naked eye. It dawned on Tommy that he was the only person in the whole wide world who knew the whereabouts of the treasure.

"Rocky Road." Tommy was startled as Carol happily thrust an ice-cream cone in his face. He looked shaken.

"What happened? Is everything all right?" Carol asked anxiously.

"Thanks, Mom. Just thinking," Tommy averted his face. He had to make a decision quickly. He hesitated, and then asked his mother the question that could change their lives.

"Mom, if you were to get an instant fortune, what would you do?" he asked hesitatingly.

"Hm, let's see. I'd fire my boss. Send you to boarding school for a year. Go to Las Vegas, double my money, and board a cruise ship for a worldwide tour. In other words, I'd go bananas, but I'll survive. Why do you ask?" Carol said good-naturedly.

"No reason! I think it's wise to earn money," Tommy was taken aback by his mother's expansive and expensive response. "Maybe if you were to get it later, it could be a comfortable retirement."

"Maybe. Why do you ask?" Carol said, licking her ice cream.

"Just a thought, Mom."

A boy zipped past on a skateboard.

"Mom, would you buy me a skateboard?"

"Yes. If you get As in math and science, just like you do in English."

"Cool! If I get an A in math, science, and history, will you buy me an iPad?"

"Sure. But you'll have to clean out the weeds in the backyard too."

"I'll try." Tommy gave the lake one last look and smiled. The mother and son walked leisurely in the sunny afternoon, licking their ice-cream cones and negotiating small chores and the pleasures of life.

CHAPTER 45

It was warm and dry in Tora Bora, the notorious part of Afghanistan, which according to many was once the hideout of Osama bin Laden. The mountains looked rugged and daunting, and the valley was full of caked mud. The sparse green vegetation reminded everyone of the treacherous terrain of that region. The gray sunset, along with the evening breeze, made the whole place look deserted. The sky looked sinister without a moon or stars.

The US Marines were cleaning up the area looking for mines and improvised explosive devices planted by insurgents. Some marines scanned the area with their high-powered binoculars and metal detectors while others moved slowly behind them, providing cover.

Suddenly, one marine noticed movement in a bushy area at a distance. He motioned to his colleagues to stop and stay silent. The marine watched a tall figure bending over in the thorny bushes.

"Halt!" one marine shouted and walked cautiously to the man in the bushes. Other soldiers in the nearby armored vehicle covered him with pointed guns.

"*Wodrega, halta sok de!*" the marine shouted in Pashto, meaning, "who's there?" The marine, still pointing his gun at the figure, came close and shouted again.

Slowly, the figure turned around. In the bright beam from the flashlight, the soldier noticed the man was likely to be in his early forties. He was emaciated, with sunken cheeks and dark circles round the eyes. He had matted, long, wavy hair that was grimy with dust. There were cuts and bruises on his face and arms. His long, dense beard was matted and reached his navel. He looked scruffy, as if he had not taken a shower in months. His clothes were tattered and soiled. His sandals were made of raw animal hide. He looked like a hermit.

He did not run or look alarmed at the sight of a gun-wielding soldier. There was something in his left hand, which he covered with his right hand, as if he was trying to hide it.

"What's in your hand?" the Marine asked sternly in Pashto, still pointing the gun at the hermit's hand. His long beard and hair meant he was likely a militant fighter. Yet his face was serene, and his body language was calm even though men in uniform surrounded him.

There had been talk among the tribal people of a blue-eyed, redheaded stranger wandering between Pakistan and the Afghanistan border. Some called him a recluse; others thought he was from another planet. Still others swore that he was an angel because he looked so peaceful. His origin remained a mystery since he never stayed in one place for long or spoke to anyone. People saw him roaming the rugged terrain staring at the summit with empty eyes in deathlike silence.

The hermit extended his clasped hands to the marine. In the glow of the sharp army flashlight, his blue eyes looked like marbles under his carrot-colored hair.

"Woderga kana walamde!" The alarmed Marine shouted a command in Pashtu, meaning "stop or I'll shoot."

"It's a female gecko." The hermit spoke softly and opened his fist just a crack, from which emerged the head of a lizard.

"You're American?" The surprised Marine lowered his gun.

The redhead looked disoriented and confused.

"What's your name?" asked the marine, searching the man for weapons.

"I...climb," the hermit responded haltingly.

"Sir, you need to come with us to the base." The hermit looked bewildered but did not resist as several marines escorted him to the armored car.

No one knew that a hell of a celebration awaited the redhead in San Felipe, California.

CPSIA information can be obtained at www.ICGtesting.com
Printed in the USA
LVOW041626131212

311547LV00007B/980/P